Weekly Reader

Children's Book Club

EDUCATION CENTER • COLUMBUS 16, OHIO

Presents

CIRCUS PARADE

STORIES OF THE BIG TOP

CIRCUS PARADE

STORIES OF THE BIG TOP

PARADE

STORIES OF THE BIG TOP

SELECTED BY

PHYLLIS R. FENNER

ILLUSTRATED BY LEE AMES

NEW YORK: ALFRED · A · KNOPF: 1954

WEEKLY READER

Children's Book Club

Edition, 1955

L.C. catalog card number: 54–9183

THIS IS A BORZOI BOOK,
PUBLISHED BY ALFRED A. KNOPF, INC.

PRINTED IN THE UNITED STATES OF AMERICA
AMERICAN BOOK–STRATFORD PRESS, INC., NEW YORK

THIS BOOK IS ESPECIALLY FOR

HELENE NICHOLS *NO*

WHO IS THE BEST PERFORMER IN HER OWN FIELD

I EVER SAW.

Special Notice to Book Club Members

★ This book is a selection of the WEEKLY READER CHILDREN'S BOOK CLUB. It was chosen for you by the Editors and Selection Committee of *My Weekly Reader*, the most famous school newspaper in the world.

Members of the WEEKLY READER CHILDREN'S BOOK CLUB receive six or more exciting books during the year — including one or more Free Bonus Books upon joining. They also receive a Membership Certificate, Club Bookmarks and regular Book Club Bulletins.

We hope you enjoy this book and that you will tell your friends about the WEEKLY READER CHILDREN'S BOOK CLUB. They will want to become members, too!

WEEKLY READER
Children's Book Club
EDUCATION CENTER, COLUMBUS 16, OHIO

Contents

CIRCUS PARADE

STORIES OF THE BIG TOP

Jenny and Her Pets

DON LANG

The little curly-haired dog yapped excitedly at the bright links of the heavy chain that lay slack on the ground. It was looped loosely around one ponderous ankle and was forged to the stout iron stake anchored in concrete just a foot away. The big elephant swayed from side to side, rocking her weight first on one forefoot and then the other, her trunk skimming the ground as it swung from right to left. Her ragged ears fanned backward and forward. The air was laden with the musty odor of the menagerie-tent.

Off in the distance a calliope played on and on. Hawkers vied with each other in shouting their wares—all pleading the cause of the elephants. "Pea—nuts! Pop—corn! You can't make friends with the elephants without your fresh roasted pea—nuts! Pop—corn!"

Up and down the long picket line the elephants all swayed

to the rhythm of the circus. The crowd which had gathered, blocking the entrance to the main tent, was for the moment more interested in the antics of the spunky little dog annoying that chain than in the elephants.

Jenny sensed this. She reached her trunk out, searching the crowd, begging. Clack! Clack! Clack! Peanuts hit their mark being tossed from every direction. Her trunk full, she doubled it under, stuffed the peanuts into her mouth and blew her pleasure.

The dog lay flat on his belly, his hind legs stretched out straight, his curled tail wagging, his front paws toying with the heavy chain. Then he rolled over on his back, twisted his head around in the dirt, grabbed the chain with his teeth, and tried his best to shake it, barking and snarling at it.

"Hey! Hey! Be quiet, will you, you good-for-nothing little whelp?"

The dog turned and looked up. It was Uncle Jed Tompkins who had shouted like that. He was sitting just inside the guard rope, leaning against the tent pole, his back to the crowd, idly tapping his bull hook against the leg of his stool. He was waiting for word to get his elephants ready for the matinee performance.

Without another bark, the dog got up and shook himself in a half-hearted effort to shake the dirt and chaff out of his long, untidy hair. Then he lay down, solemnly rested his head against the big, whitewashed forefoot of the elephant, and with a bored sigh, closed his eyes.

"Gee, mister, mightn't that elephant step on that little dog?"

"No, indeed. Don't worry!" replied the keeper turning halfway around to face a freckle-faced youngster holding onto the rope railing. "Jenny's not going to hurt him!"

The boy watched, fascinated, as the elephant gathered up a load of hay in her trunk and gently piled it on top of the dog. Then she went on swaying from side to side, in perfect time with the rest of the herd.

The boy gasped. "What's she doing covering him up like that? The poor thing will smother!"

"No, he won't smother!" assured the keeper, digging his hook into the ground with vim. He loved to talk about his elephant. "She just covers him up like that for safekeeping till she gets back from her performance!"

The boy was flabbergasted. For a moment his eyes wandered up and down the long picket line of elephants. Then coming back to Jenny and the dog once more, he asked: "Is that your dog, mister?"

The man chuckled. "What? That little pup?" he said good-naturedly. "That's *her* dog!"

"You're fooling me, mister."

"I'm not fooling you!" insisted the keeper. "But that elephant's crazy about pets." Then with a twinkle he added: "Worse than a freckle-faced boy, she is. That's how she got that pup."

"It is?"

"Sure it is. And not only that!" The man lowered his voice confidentially. "There's not an animal in the circus that's not crazy about her. That goes for the lions and tigers, too."

"Jiminy!" marveled the boy. "An elephant!"

A bustle started down at the far end of the herd. The old man got up. He draped Jenny in her gaudy silk shawl and spangles and made her ready for the parade.

With a flourish of trumpets, the band struck up a martial air. Jed unhooked the shackle chain and guided the big elephant around by the hook pressed lightly in her trunk. She gingerly withdrew her front foot as she stepped away, careful to avoid disturbing the sleeping dog under the hay, caught hold of the tail of the elephant in front of her, and the march began.

"Guess I ought to be getting in, mister, to see the show!"

It was some two years later, in Baltimore, that the little curly-haired dog died. That was a real calamity. Until then, no one had realized what the dog had meant to Jenny. He didn't even have a formal name. He had just been taken for granted. But he had been her close companion for twelve years—ever since, as a half-starved, homeless stray hanging around the railroad yards, Jenny had taken a shine to him and he had followed her to the lot. Now the loss of him broke her up completely.

For days on end Jenny stood, a sad figure, her head bowed, the end of her trunk touching the ground. She refused to eat, and took no interest in anything about the place, not even the crowds milling up and down the picket line.

The management was worried for fear they would lose her, if something wasn't done to get her mind off the dog. Over Uncle Jed's startled protests, it was finally decided to bring Albert in and chain him next to her. Albert was a killer elephant, and every elephant in the herd was scared to death of him. Perhaps Albert would act as a tonic for Jenny. Uncle Jed Tompkins pleaded with them, but his pleas fell on deaf ears.

He was sitting by Jenny, that morning, wishing there was something he could do, when down at the other end a fidgeting broke out among the elephants. There was a squeal or two. The nervousness spread up the picket line. The whole herd began fretting and tossing, bumping each other. A bull trumpeted long and loud. Then another one. Jenny didn't move, but Uncle Jed raised up off his stool to see.

They were bringing Albert down the line. The big elephant was in irons, and a keeper walked at each side of his head, their hooks prodding his trunk. Every foot was shackled, one to the other. The chains clanked as they dragged on the ground.

The bad elephant was led into place beside Jenny. His feet were chained securely to stakes. The bull boys all backed away, but remained close so that they could come to Jenny's rescue. Albert stood quietly, taking in his new surroundings. The others on the line fretted and stamped, but Albert made no effort to escape or cause trouble. He didn't even test the strength of the chains holding him. Not a bellow escaped him, not a squeal. The men were mystified. They had never seen him docile like that.

In a minute, Jenny perked up and began to take an interest in her new neighbor. Her tiny eyes sized him up, and to the amazement of all, her trunk reached over and fearlessly rested on the top of his head.

The big elephant swayed. His ears fanned. The men waited, tense, ready to go into action with swinging clubs and hooks. Albert's trunk went up in the air, hesitated, poised to strike, then gently caught hold of Jenny's trunk and clasped it in friendly fashion.

"Well, bless my soul and body!" cried Uncle Jed Tompkins. "That's just like her. She's befriended the old scoundrel!"

He was a happy man as he split a bale of hay between the two elephants. And when Jenny stole an apple out of his pocket, he took one from the other pocket and tossed it into Albert's open mouth.

The circus wended its way from city to city, from town to town, until it reached Trinidad. Jenny and Albert had become fast friends. The two elephants were never separated. When she went about tending her chores, loading and unloading the circus, setting it up and knocking it down, he teamed up with her. After many violent protests, the herd itself had finally accepted Albert on the picket line. But the job of educating him for a spot in the performing troupe was a tough one. He was still headstrong and temperamental, quick to wrath. If the slightest thing went wrong, he would fly into one of his crazy tantrums. The question would always arise whether it wasn't too risky to fool with him.

It was a sweltering hot day under canvas at Trinidad. The tent was packed. The crowd watched awed and fascinated as the elephant troupe, sixty-five trained elephants, went through their act. Behind the scenes, just on the other side of the red curtains to the entrance, a pack of greyhounds strained at their leashes as they awaited the cue for their race around the track.

Completing their first number, the elephants all moved to the front of their rings to take their bows. The whistle blew for an encore, and right then, an overanxious greyhound, eager to be the first on the track, mistook that signal for his cue. He bolted his leash and came out a-flying with a monkey dressed as a jockey on his back. The crowd whooped and shouted.

An elephant screamed. The weird and terrifying blast penetrated from one end of the circus to the other. It was Albert. Again and again, he sounded off his fury. The frightened greyhound ran through an exit and disappeared. Trunk arched and waving above his head, bellowing and blowing his anger, Albert bolted out of the arena, and plunged down the circus track, the pounding of his feet throwing up a cloud of dust and sawdust.

Pandemonium broke loose. People shrieked and yelled as the huge, bellowing beast, blind with rage, came toward them. Panic seized the other elephants and spread from ring to ring as elephants bolted, knocked over props, and squealed in wild confusion. Instantly the place was overrun with attendants and guards, armed with poles and irons, after Albert.

Suddenly, out of the milling mob, lashing right and left with her trunk, came another elephant. Jenny! Down the track she thundered after Albert. Just in time, she drove herself like a wedge between Albert and the terrified people in the stands.

Wham! Wham! Her powerful trunk beat wickedly down across the surprised elephant's head. She lashed and she thrashed as she pushed and shoved him away from the stands out onto the track.

Trembling all over from the shock of Jenny's attack, Albert made no attempt to defend himself or fight back. He just stood there and took his beating in a perfect daze. The keepers formed in a wide circle and watched, knowing better than to interfere.

When satisfied that he had been punished enough, Jenny gently turned the chastised elephant around. He grabbed her tail with his trunk and slowly she lumbered away, with Albert following meekly behind, back to the ring, where they took their usual places. The elephant act was quickly reorganized. All the elephants came into their rings and finished out their performance. The crowd was thrilled.

From then on, a great change came over Albert. Uncle Jed Tompkins had no more trouble with him. He took kindly to work and handling, and became gentle and friendly. And as the circus moved from town to town and went in and out of winter quarters with the change of seasons, under Jenny's patient and constant attention, Albert became a star performer.

But it just seemed as if the tragedies of life were forever camping on poor old Jenny's trail. One year, after a long, hard season, the show was at St. Louis. The tents had all been set up and a day's rest was the order. The weather was stifling.

Along about noon, Albert was stricken with a severe heart attack. He collapsed. His great frame crumpled in a heap as he went down. Jenny stood over him, pathetically trying her best to help him. She raised her head and trumpeted and trumpeted for Uncle Jed Tompkins to come.

Uncle Jed heard her in the mess-tent. He came running, but it was too late. He found Albert dead and Jenny down on her knees beside him, her trunk resting across his lifeless body.

Then began a battle to save Jenny's life. Again she lost all ambition, all interest in everything. For hours she stood motionless, her small eyes looking off into space, grieving for Albert. He'd been such a care to her, and now she missed him. She wouldn't eat. She couldn't be worked. Day by day, Uncle Jed watched over her failing strength and couldn't do a thing about it. Other elephants were brought in. A baby elephant! A pony! A dog! A cat! But none of them interested her.

The circus moved on to its scheduled stop at Parry Sound, Ontario. The elephants were unloaded and paraded from the train siding to the lot. Jenny was plodding along in line with the rest of the herd, paying no attention to the crowds of boys and girls who had turned out to see the unloading.

Reaching the edge of the town, the procession passed a field. Suddenly Jenny stopped. The elephant behind her and all those down the line stopped. Uncle Jed jabbed her lightly with the bull hook and slapped her trunk gently with his hand to get her going. She paid no attention. The whole parade was at a standstill. Then, casually, Jenny stepped out of line and started out across that open field.

Uncle Jed, taken by surprise, hollered at her. "Hey, Jenny!"

But she didn't hear him. She didn't want to. She just kept on going, moving at a faster gait all the time.

Out there in the center of that field, tied to a stake and grazing placidly, was a black-and-white nanny goat. Straight for the goat Jenny headed, hustling clumsily along, softly trumpeting, a trumpet of complete satisfaction.

The nanny goat looked up and spied Jenny coming. At first she was surprised and puzzled at the sight of such a huge, strange-looking visitor. But the sound of that friendly trumpeting seemed to reassure her. She stood her ground. They met, those two, the great lumbering elephant and the tiny mite of a goat, right out in the center of that field.

For a few brief moments, they stood there facing each other as if busily engaged in earnest conversation, talking it over. Bull boys swarmed all over the field to head the elephant off.

But a bargain was hastily struck. Jenny reached down, took hold of the goat's chain in her trunk and yanked the stake clear up out of the ground. Gathering the chain up in her

trunk, she hustled the nanny goat across the field and fell
in behind the parade. Both of them were conversing in perfect understanding, the elephant softly trumpeting, the
nanny goat softly bleating.

It was getting late. The menagerie-tent was up. The animals
had all been fed. Uncle Jed Tompkins was seated on his stool
tilted against a tent pole idly digging his elephant hook into
the sawdust-covered ground. Jenny stood quietly eating hay,
the first in ten days. Alongside her, grazing on the same pile,
was the black-and-white nanny goat. The pair made a picture
of contentment and ease.

"Say, mister?"

Uncle Jed glanced around in surprise. "What're you doing
in here, boy?" he asked.

"Seen anything of a goat around here?" inquired the child,
his eyes trying to take in the whole menagerie at once.

"A what?"

"A goat!" repeated the boy. "My black-and-white nanny
goat. They told me back at the police station that an elephant
stole her. And there wasn't anything they could do about it.
If a person stole it, they could do something. But there
aren't any laws in this country governing elephants."

"Now listen to me, son," said Uncle Jed, "you got to slow up
some. You know I'm an old man. And I can't hear so well
nor think as fast as I used to."

The boy was impatient. "Well, did you see anything—" He
spotted the goat. "There she is," he exclaimed, "behind that
big elephant there! Hey, Gloria! Come here." He swung
over the rope past Uncle Jed, to rescue his goat.

Uncle Jed jumped up. "Stop! Hey, boy!" he shouted in
alarm. "Come back here! That elephant will kill you sure if
you try to take her goat away."

"It's not her goat. It's mine," the boy protested indignantly, as he grabbed the goat by the chain and ran out of
the tent.

Jenny squealed and stormed. All down the picket line other elephants trumpeted and fretted. Bull boys aroused from their dozing sprang to see what was the matter.

"Trouble, Uncle Jed?" shouted a roustabout.

"Boy got his goat and gone!" answered Uncle Jed. "There's mischief to pay. Watch Jenny, so that she don't bust her chain, while I catch up to the boy!"

Outside the tent, the boy stopped to get his bearings, the goat to nibble grass. Uncle Jed soon caught up to them.

"Hey, son, hold on. Just listen to me," he pleaded.

"You can't have this goat, mister!" the boy said defiantly. "She's mine."

"You hear all that fuss back there in the tent?" asked the old man. "There's a stampede coming if I don't get this goat back to that elephant."

"Hurry up, Jed!" shouted one of the men at the entrance to the tent. "Hurry up!"

"Listen here! What do you want for her?" asked Jed.

"Five dollars!" the boy answered, without hesitation.

"Five dollars?" demurred the old man. "Why, I've seen elephants weren't half as much. But here," and he began to count from a roll of dirty, worn bills. "One! Two! Three! Four! Eh! Eh! Eh! Six! Seven! Eight! Nine! And here's another one! Ten! There's ten! All I got to my name but one. I was saving them up for a rainy day, but judging by the sounds back there, it's never going to rain any harder."

"I just need the five, mister!" said the boy, taking the bills and stuffing them in his pocket.

"Take 'em!" said the exasperated man. "Give me that goat—"

"Can I get in to see the circus, too, mister?"

"Sure. You can get in to see all four shows if you want. Anything." Uncle Jed started dragging the goat back to the tent, followed by the boy, his hand in his pocket clutching the bills.

It was evening. Quiet had been restored. The elephant and the nanny goat grazed contentedly on sweet clover hay. Old Uncle Jed Tompkins sat on his stool, tilted back against the tent pole, idly jabbing his elephant hook into the sawdust-covered ground, while he told this same boy, wide-eyed and attentive, the story of Jenny and all her pets.

Cat Man

CHARLES COOMBS

The Menagerie tent was already up. From a short distance came the shouts of the razorbacks as they quickly but systematically unloaded the gaily colored wagons from the railroad flatcars. Mixed with the shouting was the chant of the guying-out men as, rope by rope, they stretched the big top taut in hurried preparation for the afternoon show. These were but two of the sounds that formed a cacophony familiar to Jeff Ralston's ears. The acrid odor of the animals, the dusty odor of the circus lot, and the bright splashes of color added to the vibrant thrill that surged through him.

It was great to be part of it all.

"Hey, you!" a voice warned behind him. "Get away from that tiger!"

Sascha's feline ears snapped back tight against her head. Her greenish-brown eyes focused on something behind Jeff. The giant Bengal hissed menacingly through her bared fangs. Jeff's hand froze where he had been stroking the great cat's striped neck. He suppressed the sudden urge to jerk his arm out from between the bars of the cage.

"Easy, girl!" Jeff soothed. "Easy, Sascha!" He realized that despite the fact that he and the giant Bengal were friends, any sudden movement might well invite a lightning-fast slash from the startled tiger's razor-tipped claws.

During the brief moment of uncertainty on Sascha's part, Jeff pulled back to safety. He turned to look at the large, square-faced man dressed in the familiar uniform of a cat trainer.

"You—you should know better than to startle Sascha like that," Jeff accused, struggling to control his rage. "She might've taken my arm—"

"How many times I got to tell you to keep away from them tigers?" Duff Colton gestured with the lead-weighted handle of his rawhide whip. "You wanna get mauled like your old man did?"

"You still shouldn't have come up like that," Jeff insisted. "You're supposed to know cats."

"Cats. Cats! You call that Sascha a cat? She's a killer!" Duff Colton shoved past Jeff and swung the leaded whip handle between the bars of the cage, rapping the tiger sharply in the nose.

"Back, you stinker!" he yelled. Sascha roared and retreated to the far side of the cage.

Momentarily Jeff's anger flared and instinctively he charged, his fist hitting the large man with all the force of his close-packed 165 pounds. They went down under the force of Jeff's charge, but Duff Colton, bigger and more powerful than the boy, twisted astride Jeff's body and began to pommel him with his fists. Painfully, Jeff fought back from his position on the ground. He lashed out at Duff Colton's face above him. But his wrist was caught in Duff's strong grasp. He saw Duff prepare to hit him again—realized vaguely that he was powerless to avoid it, and prepared for the impact.

"Break it up!" a voice commanded sharply. A boot lashed

out and Duff Colton went sprawling in the sawdust. The boot belonged to Boss Leland, general manager and half-owner of the Park & Leland Circus. "Fine thing!" he accused. "Just great! Riling up the cats like this just before a show. Colton, you can get cleaned up. Beat it! Jeff, don't let me catch you around the cats again."

Jeff sucked in his breath. "But, Mr. Leland, I—I—"

"Keep away from the cats!"

It was almost like telling Jeff to stop breathing. He had been raised with the big cats. As long as he could remember, all of his vacations had been spent under the big top, helping his father and dreaming of the day when he, Jeff, would be working the cats. After graduation he had caught up with the Park & Leland Circus, and his father had started at once to train him to handle the famous Ralston cats.

But it hadn't been long until Jeff discovered that Duff Colton had similar ambitions for working the cats. Duff was getting tired of being a zooman; tired of all the chores that went with the job of nursemaiding the menagerie animals. He seemed suddenly attracted by the steel arena and the bright lights that went with it.

"He'll never work the Ralston cats if I can help it," Jeff's father had confided in him one day. "Duff Colton's no cat man."

But the very next week near tragedy struck during an afternoon performance in Des Moines. Jeff's dad was working a mixed act of lions and tigers. The cats were pyramiding themselves nicely when, without warning, Sascha suddenly leaped.

The big top was filled with screams, fainting women, and near panic. Alert attendants soon drove Sascha off—but not soon enough to prevent the badly crushed arm and serious lacerations that still kept Jeff's father hospitalized.

Duff Colton, into whose hands the cat act immediately fell, was all for destroying Sascha. Nor was there much opposition to his proposal. And Sascha would undoubtedly have been shot as a killer had Jeff not noted a strangely bloodshot pattern in the great striped beast's eyes.

"I tell you there's something wrong with Sascha," he pleaded with Boss Leland. "Sascha's no killer."

"Funny that you'd be wantin' to defend her, Jeff, it bein' your own dad who's fightin' for his life in the hospital," the manager had said.

"If Dad was conscious, he wouldn't let you destroy Sascha," Jeff insisted. "Something's wrong, I tell you. You've got to wait. Anyhow, they're Dad's cats."

"You're wrong there, son. The cats have belonged to the show ever since that accident to your kid sister. Your dad had to borrow some money. We took a mortgage on the cats. Sure, we still call 'em the Ralston cats—good business, see—but they ain't really your pa's cats any more, son."

That didn't alter Jeff's persistence, and he finally prevailed upon Boss Leland to postpone Sascha's sentence at least until the following day. And within twenty-four hours Jeff's observations proved valid. By mid-morning of the following day, Sascha was more dead than alive with pneumonia.

That helped account for the cat's sudden ferocity during the previous day's show. It accounted for the beast's bloodshot eyes. And it drew a new sympathy from the kinkers and the roughnecks alike. Yet not one of the performers or the workers had enough sympathy to risk ministering to the stricken animal—except Jeff.

For three days and nights, aided somewhat from the outside by Doc Carter, the circus's aged veterinarian, Jeff made hypodermic injections into the artery that ran to the tip of the feline's tail. Cautiously and soothingly he worked with the giant beast to keep an improvised pneumonia jacket on her. The fever reached its peak; then broke. Jeff talked soothingly and steadily to the Bengal. Whenever he entered the cage, Sascha raised her head warily, seemed to recognize him, and let her head back down on the sawdust.

During the evening of the fourth day, Sascha managed an

uneven purr while Jeff was in the cage. The boy pursed his own lips and blew through them in a coarse imitation of the cat's friendly sign.

"You'd better come out of there now," Doc Carter warned. "That cat'll be well enough pretty quick to do the same thing to you that she did to your dad."

During the next few weeks, the circus had continued westward with a series of one- and two-day stands. Duff Colton was still working the cats, except, of course, Sascha.

Duff's ability as a cat man was questionable. He worked them with a dogged ferocity almost equal to that of the Bengals. Every time he entered the steel arena his face was bathed in sweat, and he overemployed the whip. He showed little affection for the tigers, and was seldom seen around the dens between performances. It seemed strange to Jeff that Duff Colton had ever wanted the cat act. Undoubtedly, the man had been blinded by the glamour of the steel arena, for he seemed to dislike working the creatures.

Sascha hadn't been out of her rolling den since her illness. And had it not been for the protesting letters Jeff's father continued to send Boss Leland from the hospital, Sascha would long since have been done away with or donated to some local zoo, few of which could afford to feed her the twenty pounds of fresh meat she required daily. So Sascha went along with the circus.

When it became apparent that Jeff's father would not return to the show for at least another season, and perhaps longer, Jeff approached Boss Leland for permission to start working the cats during part of each rehearsal period. But his request was politely refused.

"Someday, maybe," Boss Leland encouraged, "but you're pretty young, kid. You got a lot to learn about tigers before you try working in the steel arena. Maybe someday, huh?"

But "someday" would be too late, Jeff knew. Duff Colton was already remolding the act; eliminating some of the stunts which he seemed to consider particularly hazardous to his own welfare. Duff's sole control over the cats was based on fear. True, as Jeff knew, fear was a requisite in maintaining the tigers' respect. But he also knew that an element of trust was essential between man and animal in order to accomplish a smooth act inside the steel arena.

Soon, Jeff thought soberly, the last vestige of the carefully worked-out and once-famous Ralston routine would be gone. Jeff was surprised that Boss Leland, usually a perfectionist, would allow the act to slip the way it had since Duff Colton took it over.

It was a warm summer night and the gaily decorated big top was packed with the eager and excited populace of King City. The cat act had just opened the show, drawing what seemed to Jeff a rather polite round of applause. The tractors had pulled the rolling dens out of the tent into the circus back yard. Inside the tent the roustabouts were hastily dismantling the linked steel arena. Out along the railroad siding the workmen were busily loading the cook tent, the animal tent, and the greater portion of the wild animals onto the cars that made up the circus train's first section. As soon as the performance was finished, the Flying Squadron would be all ready to move out through the night toward the next day's stand.

The tinny blare of the band seeped through the canvas side-walls as Jeff helped load the rolling kitchens onto the flatcars. Suddenly, from forward along the train came the splintering crash of wood. Startled shouts sounded over the confusion, but were quickly suppressed.

As Jeff broke into a run toward the front of the train he knew that whatever had happened to cause that crash of sound had been serious.

Someone sped past Jeff. "Better go back, kid," he panted. "Tiger's loose!"

Jeff paused a moment; then moved cautiously forward. He was soon near enough to discern some of the work crew hanging to telephone poles or perched on various high vantage points of safety. He also saw the cage lying at a steep angle, one end on the ground and one end still resting on the bed of the flatcar. He saw how the wheels had slipped from the ramp running between the cars. He saw how one barred end of the cage—the end resting on the ground—had burst open at the impact.

"Scram, kid!" a workman cried urgently from a nearby telephone pole. "It's the killer that got away! Sascha!"

"Sascha!" A chill surged along Jeff's spine. "Where is she?"

"Last I saw her," a voice volunteered from the semi-darkness, "she was headed toward that orchard out there the other side of the tracks. But you never know what them cats are goin' to do. She might've doubled back and—and maybe she's under one of them flatcars right now!"

Boss Leland, Duff Colton, and several others came running up, carrying rifles and strong-beamed flashlights.

"We're going after her," the circus manager said quickly. "See that this doesn't leak into the big tent. Don't want any riots on our hands."

Jeff quickly recalled costly circus panics that his father had told him about. "You—you're not going to shoot Sascha?" he said anxiously.

"Can't take any chances, Jeff," Boss Leland replied. "You fellows with the rifles spread out in pairs and start through the orchard. If you see her, be sure you make your shots count or—hey, Colton, what's the matter with you?"

Jeff saw then how Duff Colton was edging away; saw the pastiness of the trainer's face in the dim light.

"I—I'd better stay here," he managed, "in case Sascha should double back and—well, tigers often come back to familiar places, you know, and—"

"Yeah, yeah, I think you better stay," Boss Leland snapped, scowling at him. "And maybe you better find a place to hide while you're at it!"

Without a word Duff Colton walked back toward the lighted tent.

The searching beams of the flashlights soon disappeared into the orchard. Cautiously, the workmen climbed down, raised the empty cage to its proper position on the flatcar and watchfully resumed their labor. Jeff went back into the big top, where the show was reaching the mid-point. Although word had quickly passed among the performers, not a single person in the packed bleachers was even remotely aware that a cat was loose.

A half-hour passed. A half-hour during which Jeff busied himself breaking down and setting up the ring trappings for each new act. He tried to keep busy enough not to think of what might be happening outside in the darkness, as men with rifles stalked the tawny Sascha.

Then it came—a single sharp report—like someone breaking a dry stick over his knee. An involuntary sob shook Jeff. He bit down hard on his lower lip; felt it tremble against his teeth.

"All I hope is that they got her with that shot," Duff Colton said hoarsely.

Jeff turned away, fighting down the rage that seethed within him.

The band was blaring out its brassy fanfare for the aerial act, the final feature of the show. At his post near one of the trapeze guy-wires, Jeff was still thinking of Sascha, of how he could break the news to his father. For years Sascha had been his dad's favorite tiger.

Duff Colton loitered nearby, apparently much more at ease since hearing the single rifleshot.

Jeff thought it was strange that a clown should suddenly come rushing in through the performers' exit. He quickly recognized him as Perry Prince, king of the bulbous-nosed joeys. Perry shot nervous glances around, spotted Jeff, and rushed over to him. Despite the thick greasepaint, Jeff immediately saw the fear in the clown's eyes.

"It's Sascha!" Perry Prince shot a quick glance back over his shoulder. "I just saw her coming out from under a wagon.

She's headed this way, kid! Where's the boss? Get a gun! Hey, Duff, you—"

Duff Colton had already come over. At hearing the clown's words, his face suddenly blanched. "But that shot?"

"Musta missed," the clown said. "Hurry up. You better do somethin'! If that cat—" Perry Prince's words trailed off. His eyes widened.

Staring past him, Jeff saw Sascha move into sight out of the dark shadows beyond the performers' exit. The great Bengal stalked forward in a low crouch, swaying her head slowly from side to side.

"Beat it!" Duff Colton's hoarse whisper was filled with fear. "Let's get out of here! That—that cat's on the prod!"

"Wait, Duff!" Jeff said quickly. "Stand still! Want to start a panic?"

But the cat trainer had already moved to a position where one of the big tent poles offered him a measure of protection.

"Better beat it!" Perry Prince said, edging away. "I don't want any truck with that killer."

"Stand still, you fool!" Jeff stopped him with his voice. "Don't run!" His eyes and mind were quickly sizing up the situation, groping—groping. He fought back the natural impulse to follow Duff Colton's lead and find some kind of protection. But at any cost, even at the risk of his own life, he must prevent the people in the bleachers from knowing that danger threatened them.

"Perry. Quick!" Jeff grabbed the clown's arm. "Get some help. Roll a chute out here and an arena cage . . . slow, easy. Don't get Sascha excited."

"But—"

"Go on!" Jeff commanded. "Go on!"

The clown moved quietly away, and Jeff could only hope that he wasn't following Duff Colton's lead.

"Sascha!" Jeff called. "Sascha!"

The tiger turned her head slowly and fastened her greenish-brown eyes on Jeff. Even at the distance Jeff could see the frightened uncertainty in the beast's actions. Without taking his eyes off the Bengal, Jeff eased over beside the ringmaster, who stood with his whip held loosely in his hand—stood with beads of sweat pebbling his forehead—paralyzed at the sight of the approaching tiger.

"Quick, Lou," Jeff whispered, indicating the walking microphone held in the ringmaster's other trembling hand. "Tell 'em this is a special tiger act. Hold up the trapeze stunt."

"Hey, kid, you can't—"

But Jeff wasn't paying any attention. Sascha had moved into full view under the brilliant arc lights. Now Jeff saw the large blotch of red on Sascha's right shoulder, and again fought desperately against the impulse to turn and run for freedom. Sascha was wounded! Jeff saw now the crazed, feverish look in her eyes.

"Don't move!" Jeff called tensely to a panic-faced usher. "Don't move or she'll kill you!"

The ringmaster hadn't had time to make his announcement. The band suddenly went mute. Everything under the big top suddenly froze into immobility. The arena ached with silence, a silence that could at any moment transform into a terror-ridden panic. It was too late now for any pretense.

One scream, one person suddenly breaking for freedom—would create complete havoc.

Jeff took the whip from the ringmaster's trembling hand. "Sascha!" He moved forward, popped the whip to center the tiger's attention: "Come on. Sascha!"

The great Bengal hissed and crouched back on her haunches. She lashed out uncertainly at the whip. Jeff wondered if Sascha, in her wounded state, even recognized him.

"Easy, Sascha, easy. Come on, girl," Jeff petted her with his words, moving slowly backward as she came on. Her mammoth striped head swayed back and forth with pain and uncertainty. Jeff popped the whip again when Sascha's attention was diverted by a group of laborers who started to move away, unable to hold their positions any longer.

"Stick to me, Sascha," he coaxed. He simulated a purr by blowing through loosely pursed lips.

Sascha hesitated, as though she might be recalling similar soft tones and similar purrs from the past when she was sick or hurt.

"Come on, Sascha. We've been through worse than this together." Beyond the crouched animal, Jeff caught a quick glimpse of Boss Leland and the rest of the searching party. They stood transfixed by the scene taking place before their eyes.

Jeff hazarded a quick glance behind him—saw that Perry Prince had come through, and that a cage and a chute had been moved in and made ready to receive the cat.

Watching Sascha's wandering, pain-filled eyes, Jeff realized that he was beginning to lose control of the Bengal's attention. Once that was lost, once Sascha sensed the fear around her, anything might happen. And the silence, the complete absence of any movement, was mute testimony that everyone inside the big top was putting his trust in Jeff's ability to control the loose tiger.

Sascha stopped and licked her wound, as though the pain was setting in stronger. She swung her feverish eyes around, focused for a moment on the fear-paralyzed ringmaster.

Jeff knew that he would have to act fast now—act and hope.

"Sascha!" he shouted, turning and snapping the whip at the opening of the chute. "Sascha! In, girl!"

Then he shifted to one side and snapped the whip sharply over the Bengal's head.

"In, Sascha, in!"

The tiger looked at Jeff a moment. She started to bare her fangs in a vicious snarl. Then she seemed to realize that Jeff was still her friend, that Jeff had nothing to do with the pain in her shoulder. With a halfhearted roar, she rose up and lashed out almost playfully at the whip. Just as she would in a rehearsal of the act. Jeff jerked the whip away, and popped it quickly against Sascha's rearing head.

"In, Sascha, girl!" He popped the whip again. "In!"

Sascha seemed to catch the cue now. She took three quick steps toward the chute; then stopped and eyed Jeff uncertainly. Jeff held his stare into the Bengal's eyes.

Sascha swung her head away, and rushed into the chute. Instantly, Jeff dropped the whip and slammed the barred door of the small cage.

"Good girl, Sascha," he breathed. "Good girl!"

Sascha blinked back through the bars, as though she was glad to be home again.

There was a long moment when the only sound was the sucking in of starved breath. Then the tent thundered with applause. Jeff wanted desperately to sink down onto the sawdust and just sit there and wait for his strength to return. But he stood and forced a smile onto his sweating face, as a rush of humanity, led by Boss Leland, swarmed in on him.

"No one else in the world could have controlled that wounded cat!" Doc Carter said admiringly.

"Nor the crowd."

"Sascha and I got pretty well acquainted"—Jeff smiled—"back when she had pneumonia. She remembered. But it took her a little while. She's hurt. I'm going to help her."

"She's your cat if you want, Jeff." Boss Leland beamed. "They're all yours, if you want them. But you got to work them for me. No one else."

Jeff looked up. "You mean that I—"

"I mean that I know a real cat man when I see one. And, come to think of it, I've never known anyone who could work the Ralston cats like a Ralston. Hey, Jeff, where you goin'?"

"I've got a wire to send to my dad," Jeff said, grinning happily, as he backed through the crowd. "A long wire!"

Tinker of the Big Top

ESTHER VAN SCIVER

Tinker, the newest circus monkey, sat huddled up on his perch. Except for his bright, brown eyes, which were like shiny buttons, and his long, curling tail, the little monkey looked like a soft ball of brown fur. You would never have guessed that Tinker was unhappy, but he was.

He sat there alone in his cage and felt very sorry for himself. He thought of how frightened he had been when the hunters had taken him and carried him away from his tree-top home in the green jungles of South America. He remembered how unhappy he had been during the long sea journey when the ship had rolled and tossed in the storm. He thought of how he had missed his mother and his brothers and sisters. And he remembered how strange he had felt when he was sold to the circus and found himself in a cage, with hundreds of people looking at him and laughing.

[28]

But none of those things had made him feel as homesick as he felt now. The other monkeys all had something to do in the circus. Some rode in the pony races, others went into the arena with the clowns and made the children clap their hands. And one monkey rode on top of an elephant's head in the parade.

Tinker sat huddled up on his perch like a soft brown ball and wished that he could swing in a tree again. He did not know it was just because he was new that he was being left in his cage. Dan Field, the head animal man, wanted the monkey to feel at home among the bright lights, the people, and all the noise and excitement, before trying to teach him any tricks.

From town to town the circus traveled, and Tinker grew used to the Big Show. His cage was kept clean and there was always plenty to eat—bananas, oranges, sweet potatoes, and a pan of fresh, warm milk, morning and night.

Soon he learned to enjoy the children who watched him. He laughed when he swung from his perch to the bars of his cage and back again. He found that they liked to see him jump up and down on his perch and clap his hands as they did. He learned, too, that the boys and girls loved to see him swing by his tail.

One afternoon, while Tinker was amusing the children with his tricks, he saw that Dan Field was watching him closely. And when the people had all gone into the Big Top to see the show, the head animal man called Toto, the best clown, and together they came and stood beside Tinker's cage.

Dan poked his finger through the bars and said: "Hello there, Tinker." Tinker looked up and chattered brightly as he grabbed Dan's finger in his paw.

Dan turned to Toto and said: "Toto, I think Tinker is ready to go into the show. You take him out tomorrow and try him in the pony races."

Next day, as soon as the Big Top was up and the trains and

trucks were unloaded, Toto came to Tinker's cage. He opened the door and reached in to take the little monkey. For a minute Tinker hung back. Then he jumped into Toto's arms and held tight. Toto put a leather belt around Tinker's body and snapped a long chain to it. Then he took Tinker to the Big Top where some of the performers were riding around.

Toto put Tinker on the back of one of the ponies and led the pony around the arena. As long as Toto held on to Tinker's belt, the monkey was quiet. But as soon as Toto let go, Tinker began to chatter and cry.

Every day for two weeks Toto tried to teach Tinker to ride the pony. But it was no use. Tinker was always afraid. At last Toto went to Dan Field and said: "It's no use, Dan. That monkey just can't learn to ride."

"How about trying him in the clown act?" Dan asked.

Toto tried to teach Tinker to roll and tumble and dance as the other monkeys in the clown act did. But try as he would, he could not get Tinker to learn. So Toto went to Dan again and said: "Dan, I'm afraid we're just throwing away our time on Tinker. I don't believe he'll ever learn to perform."

"I'll tell you," said Dan, "take Tinker into the Big Top this afternoon at show time and try him out there."

That afternoon Toto put a little green velvet suit on Tinker and took him to the Big Top at show time. He put Tinker on a perch just inside the tent and fastened his chain to the post. "Well, old fellow," said Toto, "this is your last chance."

Then the drums rolled long and loud and the band began to play swinging music. Tinker looked toward the center ring where two handsome men and a lovely lady were bowing this way and that, while everyone clapped and shouted: "The Flying Concelles! The Flying Concelles! Hurrah!"

Up, up, up the ropes, hand over hand, climbed the Flying Concelles. First the lovely lady, then the handsome men. Close to the roof they climbed. As Tinker watched, his brown eyes grew brighter and brighter. Then as the three began to fly through the air, to turn and twist, to swing back and forth

from one trapeze to another, Tinker grew excited. Here was something he understood. He put his tiny brown hands up over his eyes and dreamed of himself, swinging back and forth, flying through the air, high, high up against the great white tent.

When it was time for him to go into the arena with the clowns, he hardly knew what was happening. Suddenly he saw that he was out in front of a whole tent full of people. There was noise and music, laughing and clapping. He felt strange and lost down on the ground. He looked this way and that. He saw Toto.

Straight for the clown's legs he flew. Quickly he scrambled up to Toto's shoulder, chattering and crying.

It seemed a long time before he found himself back in his own cage. How glad he was to be there! But Toto and Dan were standing near by, and he heard the clown say: "There is no use working with him. He'll never be a performer."

"I guess you're right," said Dan. "But I can't understand it. He seems bright enough. We'll just have to keep him in the animal tent until we can trade him off."

The little monkey had something to think about. He would show them what real flying tricks were! It was easy to forget that he was lonely and homesick when he thought of himself high up against the roof of the Big Top, swinging as if he were in his jungle treetop. Every day he would try the door of his cage, hoping to find it unlocked. But it never was.

One morning when the animal train was being unloaded, a heavy pole fell against Tinker's cage. Tinker's bright eyes saw that one of the bars was bent, just a little. He could hardly wait to try it. As soon as it was dark, he squeezed and wriggled, but he could not get out. The cage bar was not bent enough.

The next day Tinker felt very unhappy. He felt that he would never get a chance to swing on the trapeze. He huddled on his perch and put his little paws over his eyes. Then he heard Dan and Toto talking.

"We'll let Tinker go in this lot," Dan was saying. "Frank Black has a fine brown bear he wants to trade off for a monkey and two ponies."

"Yes, we might as well get rid of him," answered Toto. "We can't teach him anything." Then Dan and Toto went away.

Fiercely, the monkey began to wriggle his way through the bars. If he rubbed all the fur off his back, he was going to get through. His leg and shoulder hurt, but Tinker was too excited to care. He dropped quickly to the ground and kept in the shadows until he reached the empty Big Top. He slipped under the tent side and peered out from beneath a seat.

Suddenly he drew back. His heart began to beat hard and fast. Tinker heard his name called.

It was Dan Field calling. "Tinker! Where is that monkey?"

Then Toto's voice reached Tinker's ears, too. "Come to Toto, Tinker! Come, Tinker, Tinker, Tinker!"

Louder and closer came the voices. Tinker huddled back into the darkest shadows.

Dan's voice shouted out almost above him. "We have to find that monkey. Frank Black will be here with the brown bear after the show this afternoon. Hey, Tinker!"

Tinker was almost afraid to breathe. He thought surely that Dan would reach down and pick him up. He peered out again and saw that the men had passed by without seeing him.

The little monkey drew a deep breath. Once again he peered out. The Big Top was dim and still. The rows and rows of seats were empty and waiting. The ropes and wires swung against the roof of the great tent. Everything was ready for the next show. In another hour the tent would be filled.

Now Tinker had the whole place to himself. He darted across the arena to the center ring and to the ropes which held the trapezes high in the air. Then, in a flash, the little monkey fairly flew up, up, up the ropes until he found himself on a small platform close to the roof.

He reached out a small hairy hand and touched the nearest trapeze. He chirruped softly to himself. From ropes to bar and from bar to trapeze, he flew. Then he sat and dreamed happily in the tent until show time.

He awoke with a start when the bright lights came on. He jumped from the tiny platform to a trapeze. The band began to play loud, marching music, and Tinker's heart sang. He loved the drums and the trumpets.

No one noticed the small brown ball of fur perched so high among the ropes. The grand parade around the arena began, led by the ringmaster. The show was on, and Tinker sat watching, high against the roof. He saw the clowns and the tumblers, the horseback riders and the tightrope walkers.

Then the lights began to dim. Tinker's heart beat high as the lights went off, then on, to show the Flying Concelles bowing and smiling. The band played again the swinging music, and then the Flying Concelles were high in the air, ready to begin their act.

One of the handsome men stood on the tiny platform. He reached for the trapeze. But as it swung out across space with a small brown monkey hanging to it, the lovely lady gave a sharp little scream.

In a moment, all the people, even the Flying Concelles were watching Tinker. Never before had they seen such trapeze tricks. Tinker swung back and forth, back and forth. He twisted and turned, he hung by one hand, then by one toe. He hung by his tail, and the children screamed with glee. He flew from one trapeze to another and caught the narrow bar by a hair's breadth. The people were breathless. Every moment they thought that the tiny monkey would fall to the ground. But he went on, swinging back and forth.

Tinker had not spent all those happy jungle days on the vines and treetops without learning tricks which even the Concelles had never thought of. No one knows how long Tinker would have gone on flying and swinging up there, for he was having a wonderful time, and so was the crowd. But

the lovely lady saw her chance at last and caught the rope
with one hand. In a moment, Tinker was in her arms.

"Bow, Tinker, bow!" she whispered to him as she stood him
beside her on the platform.

Tinker jumped up and down and clapped his hairy little
hands together. A great roar of applause filled the Big Top.
The children shouted: "More, more, more!" and the applause
grew.

Then as Tinker was lowered to the center ring by a rope,
the boys and girls, and the grownups, too, stood up and
cheered and cheered. Toto stood close to the rope. He held
out his arms and Tinker jumped into them.

At the door of the Big Top stood Dan Field waiting for
Toto. He had heard the cheers and the laughter and the applause and had come to see what it was all about.

As Toto came out carrying Tinker, Dan called to him:
"Well, this is a fine how-de-do! It's a good thing Frank Black
is here waiting for this runaway. Pack him right off!"

"Wait, Dan, wait," said the clown. "Didn't you hear that
applause?"

"Yes, and the laughing and the cheering?" asked the ringmaster, who had hurried out, too.

"It would be a shame to throw away an act like that," said
Toto. "It's a special."

"The children loved it," added the ringmaster.

"Hmm, hmm, well, now!" growled the animal man.

"Why, Tinker stopped the show!" said Toto.

"He did, indeed!" cried the ringmaster. "He's a special!"

"Well, I suppose—" said Dan.

"Then it is all settled," said Toto happily.

"*Tinker, the Only Monkey Trapeze-Star in the World!*—
how does that sound?" asked the ringmaster.

Tinker chirruped. He did not know whether he had been
good or bad. He held his hands together and looked up at
Toto with bright, beady eyes.

"It's all right, Tinker, old fellow," said the clown.

Tinker was not quite sure just what all this talk meant. But he knows now. At each performance a very happy and clever monkey, who is not a bit homesick, does a special flying-trapeze act for his friends, the children.

Breakfast with a Hero

CAROL RYRIE BRINK

Jenny, do my curls look like wienerwursts?"

Ardeth stood in front of the mirror in a full white nightgown with frills at neck and sleeves, and gazed sadly at her reflection. She saw a short and rather plump girl of ten years, with red cheeks, round blue eyes which always seemed surprised, and reddish-brown hair that curled in tight, tubular ringlets on either side of her face. She had never thought of it before today, but perhaps the Dawlish boys were right and her curls *did* look like wienerwursts. Behind herself Ardeth could see Jenny, the housekeeper, a very large person who moved slowly and sighed often. Jenny was brushing the accused curls about her finger, and she snorted impatiently.

"Wienerwursts!" she cried. "The idea! It's them Dawlish boys putting ideas into your head again. They always have their noses in other people's business. It's just as the old saying goes, the minister's boys are always the worst scamps in town."

"They aren't scamps," protested Ardeth, "and maybe my curls *do* look like wieners."

"You'd believe that the end of your nose was green if the Dawlish boys told you so," said Jenny indignantly. "They've been here only ten days now, and they've already got you into more scrapes than you was into all the rest of the year by yourself—and you such a nice little girl, too."

"I'm not a nice little girl," protested Ardeth, shaking her curls out of Jenny's grasp.

"Listen to you now!" cried Jenny. "You *was* a nice little girl until the new minister arrived. His wife looks like a saint and he preaches hell-fire as well as old Reverend Trimble ever did, but them boys! They're lost souls, sure enough!"

"It wasn't Martin's fault I fell off the picket fence and tore my pink dress," said Ardeth. "He just said girls couldn't walk picket fences and I had to show him. And Henry didn't mean to drown the Smiths' kitten. He was trying to teach it to swim, and he gave it a wonderful funeral, and—"

"I've heard all that before," said Jenny. "You get to bed now, so you'll be rested for the circus parade tomorrow."

"Jenny, I've told you three times already that it isn't a circus. It's Buffalo Bill's *Wild West*."

"It's all one to me," said Jenny. "Sawdust and smell and horses going around in a ring. Whatever fancy name you want to call it, it's a circus to *me*."

"All right," said Ardeth. There was no use arguing with Jenny.

"And mark my words," added Jenny, "no good ever came out of a minister's boys. It's 'out of the frying pan into the fire' with them. You better have nothing more to do with them."

"Is that orders or advice?" asked Ardeth as she climbed into bed.

"Advice," said Jenny, "good, sensible advice, that's what it is!"

"Because, if it's advice, I don't really have to take it unless I think best, do I?"

"You go to sleep, miss," said Jenny tartly. "The idea!"

Sighing a great deal, Jenny got herself halfway down the stairs when Ardeth called. The lonely summer night was closing in around her and she liked to cling to human contacts as long as she could.

"Jenny! Isn't Papa home yet?"

"No, he's out on that case still. Old Mrs. Haines was took bad with her heart."

"Who'll kiss me good night?"

"Well, I will," said Jenny crossly, retracing her steps with more heavy sighing.

"I'm sorry to make you come up again, Jenny," said Ardeth gently.

"I should think you would be," complained Jenny.

But her cheek was soft and warm and smelled of face powder; and Ardeth knew that she was like her biscuits, better than they looked.

Ardeth cuddled down in bed and said very earnestly to herself: "I'm going to wake up at four. I'm going to wake up at four. One—two—three—four. I'm going to wake up at four."

This almost always worked if she thought hard enough about it just before going to sleep, and then there would be the whistles of the show train to help wake her—and Martin and Henry! It was impossible that *they* would oversleep. To Ardeth it seemed that Martin and Henry Dawlish could do anything they wished, short of magic. Although why they should stop at magic, she really didn't know, for they had completely captivated her. Something novel and entertaining was always going on around the Dawlish boys. There was never a dull moment.

Before the new minister's family had arrived, that summer in the early 1900's, there had often been dull moments for Ardeth. Her father was a busy country doctor, a quiet man even when he was at home; her mother had been dead five years; and Mattie, her school chum, lived six blocks away. Ardeth had been the only child in the block until the new minister moved into the Presbyterian manse across the alley. As long as Ardeth could remember, the manse had been occupied by the very old Reverend Mr. Trimble and his very much older sister, Miss Trimble; and the only times she had ever set foot inside its high white picket fence were the rare and painful occasions upon which Miss Trimble had asked her to tea.

But this spring old Reverend Mr. Trimble had retired, and there had been moving and cleaning and just a little fresh paint; and the Ladies' Aid, under the direction of Miss Emily Skip, had taken up a collection of not-too-much-used curtains for the windows; and somebody had donated a slightly worn red plush love seat, and someone else an almost new garden hose, and someone else a large Chinese umbrella stand that was only a little cracked on the side next to the wall. And then one day the station hack had driven up with the new minister's family. Ardeth had seen it arrive, and almost before it stopped, two boys had jumped out and begun to explore. In no time at all their blond, curly heads appeared over the top of the picket fence, looking across the alley into Ardeth's yard. Their round, angelic faces were like the bodiless cherubim which are seen floating on clouds in old-fashioned pictures.

"Hello! What's *your* name?" asked Martin, who was eleven; and Henry, who was nine, had asked: "Are you the only kid in the block?"

Well, life had waked up after that. For ten delightful days now Ardeth had shared the life of exciting adventure which always surrounded the Dawlish boys. There were two reasons why they took Ardeth at once into bosom confidence. In the first place, the Dawlish boys were not snobs. They liked everyone they met, even girls, and Ardeth, being next door and the only child in the block, came handy. In the second place, Ardeth had a Shetland pony and she knew how to saddle it, harness it, ride it, and drive it. The minister's boys had never owned a horse, although to do so was their highest ambition. In all their daydreams they saw themselves mounted on dashing horses with flying manes and tails; and the fact that the doctor's little girl owned a pony made them respect her very highly, even if her curls did look like wienerwursts.

About ten minutes to four, in that darkest time before the dawn, the first whistle of the *Wild West* train sounded down the valley. The whistle of a show train is like no other train whistle in the world. Just what the difference is it would be hard to say, but there is something more shrill, more wild and strange about the whistle of the show train. There is a hint of the calliope in it, something of the hooting of the clowns and the trumpeting of the elephants and the yahooing of the cowboys. Ardeth turned over in bed and flung her arms out over the covers, but it was hard to wake up.

The whistle sounded again and again, coming nearer up the valley among the western hills. Ardeth stirred restlessly, and then a shower of pebbles struck her window and brought her wide awake. She sat up in bed in a fright.

"Hey, Wienerwursts!" called a guarded voice from below her window.

Ardeth sprang out of bed and ran to the window. Below her on the lawn were the shadowy forms of Martin and Henry Dawlish.

"Hurry up!" hissed Martin. "It's nearly in. We'll miss the fun."

"Don't go without me," begged Ardeth.

She flung on her clothes any which way, shivering with

excitement. Every summer as long as she could remember she had gone to see the circus or the *Wild West* show and the parade, dressed in her best starched pink chambray, all washed and curled, and holding onto Jenny's large, perspiring hand. But she had never thought of seeing a show *unload* before she knew the minister's boys.

Ardeth didn't stop to wash her face or do her teeth or hair, but, when she had put on her clothes, she climbed out of the window and went down the morning-glory trellis. This was one of the chief conveniences of Ardeth's room—the morning-glory trellis came right up to her window like a little ladder.

In a moment she was hurrying down the dark street between Martin and Henry. The street seemed all unfamiliar at this time of day, and Ardeth felt a cold lump of excitement at the pit of her stomach. The whistle of the Wild West train shrieked twice from the other side of town.

"It's in!" said Martin. "It's in!"

Yes, there stood the engine, panting and puffing, beside the railway station. The swaying light of lanterns fell on dark, hurrying figures, on crates and carts, on the name of the town printed in large white letters on the side of the station—WARSAW JUNCTION. Men were shouting and pushing hand trucks or adjusting gangplanks to car doors. There was a smell of horses and animals and unknown things; there were unexpected noises: a dull roaring, a shrill neighing, and the sharp hiss of escaping steam.

Ardeth felt suddenly that she must hold onto someone or something or she would be swept away and lost forever. But Martin and Henry were not much for holding hands, and the best she could do was the tail of Martin's jacket.

"Jiminy Christmas!" said Martin. "It's all right. We got here in time to see it all."

"In time to see it all!" echoed Henry fervently. "Where's Buffalo Bill, Martin? I want to see Buffalo Bill."

"Well, hold your horses, Henry. He'll be along," said Martin.

"We shook hands with Buffalo Bill last year in Montana in our last pastorate," said Henry.

Ardeth had heard this several times before, but it always thrilled her. "Do you think he'll remember you?" she asked.

"I'll bet he will," said Henry confidently.

Now the big workhorses were being unloaded and they were set to work, pulling the heavy, creaking wagons full of poles and canvas to the meadow beyond the station where circuses and shows always pitched their tents.

Martin and Henry ran here and there trying to see everything. It was bad enough trying to see everything that went on in the three rings of the show during the performance, but this was even worse. Things were being unloaded from all the cars, wagons were being assembled, cowboys and Indians were driving oxen and leading rearing, neighing ponies. Over in the meadow, Indian tepees were being pitched; in the midst of the field, the enormous show tent was going up, to the accompaniment of shouts and cries, grunts and swearing.

"Goodness, such awful language!" said Ardeth.

"They're all good Bible words," said Martin, "only they put them in the wrong places."

"Where's Buffalo Bill?" asked Henry of everyone he met. The answer was usually: "Out of the way, kid. Gangway! You're going to get hit." But finally someone said: "Colonel Cody will be in on the next train, kid. Look out for your head now, here comes another pole."

In all of her starched-chambray and neatly curled life, Ardeth had never been so excited and pleased. The sky grew rosy pink over the meadow with its jumbled masses of canvas. The second train came in with a hooting whistle and was shunted onto a side track for unloading. Cowboys and Indians streamed out of it and began unloading more spotted ponies and bronchos and cages of buffalo and bear. Yes, and there was the famous Deadwood coach, but no Buffalo Bill.

The rosy pink grew yellow and then white, and presently it

was broad day; but if she was hungry Ardeth didn't know it, and she had entirely forgotten for the moment that such people as Jenny and her father existed.

"Where's Buffalo Bill?" Henry was still plaintively asking.

"Oh, dry up. We'll find him," said Martin kindly. "Let's go and see them have their breakfasts now."

"Breakfasts?" asked Ardeth. "Do they eat?"

"Sure. You can't move shows and do trick riding and shooting, and broncho busting, without food, you know," said Martin patiently.

The first tent to be completely set up was the dining-tent. Stoves were already installed and smoking pungently on the morning air, and a smell of frying ham, bacon, buckwheat cakes, and coffee went forth invitingly across the meadow. The Dawlish boys' noses were excellent guides in the matter of food. In a few moments the three stood in a row by the open flap of the tent watching the cooks in their greasy white caps and aprons making the show's breakfast. To Ardeth's surprise and delight, she saw that they fried their ham and flipped their pancakes right on the tops of the stoves without the bother of frying pan or skillet. The *Wild West* people came in as they found time and sat down to long wooden tables without tablecloths. It was like a picnic every day. There was a girl there in divided skirt and cowboy hat who might have been Annie Oakley, the sure-fire shot, herself; and there were Indians, too, eating ham and eggs as peacefully as white men. Just opposite the children sat a cowboy with a purple shirt and a ten-gallon hat, and he was reading a paper-covered book with a red-and-blue-and-green picture on the front of horsemen holding up a train. The book was called *The Life and Death of Jesse James, the Outlaw.*

Martin sniffed the air appreciatively.

"I sure would like some breakfast," he said regretfully, "but I can't spare the time to go home and get it."

"Oh, no," said Ardeth. "Let's not go home!"

Just then Henry, whose eyes had been roving in search of just one person, let out a whoop of delight and began to run.

"Buffalo Bill!" he yelled.

Across the trampled meadow from the main tent cantered a white horse carrying a very erect rider with a white imperial and long white hair which fluttered in the wind beneath his wide-brimmed hat. Colonel William Cody, the Indian fighter, the buffalo killer, the scout, and now in his latter years the showman and idol of small boys the country over, was riding in to get his breakfast.

"It's him!" said Martin. "It sure is!"

Henry ran on like one possessed, his arms spread wide, shouting: "Buffalo Bill, you 'member me? I shook hands with you last year in Mon—"

The horse was coming faster than Henry realized, and frightened by a blowing paper, it swerved suddenly toward him and knocked him over. He rolled over and over on the dusty grass, and lay still. Ardeth screamed and Martin began to run. The old scout reined in his horse and cantered back. A little crowd began to gather. For a moment Henry lay quiet, his face white against the trampled dog fennel and clover. Buffalo Bill sprang off his horse and bent over him.

"Henry!" called Martin. "Henry! Henry!"

Then Henry sat up, shaking his head as if to rid himself of the fog that clouded his vision.

"—last year in Montana in our last pastorate," he finished.

"Well, now, young feller, you kind of ran amuck, didn't you?" said Colonel Cody.

"He was so glad to see you," explained Martin, coming up with Ardeth. "Are you all right, Henry?"

"Sure," said Henry, still a little dazed and gazing around at the gathering crowd to see what was bringing them.

"His head's pretty tough," said Martin to Buffalo Bill. "Once he got it caught in a cider press, but nothing happened. Mama says he's got the Dawlish skull—and you can't crack it."

"He'd make a good Indian fighter," said the old scout.

"You bet I would!" said Henry, beginning to take an interest in the conversation.

"Can you stand up?" asked the Colonel. "You don't hurt anywhere, eh? No bones broken?" Henry stood up and dusted himself off.

"I reckon I'm all here," he said.

"What's all this about your last pastorate?"

"Me and Martin shook your hand then. Do you remember?"

"Well, I'm an old man, now, bud. My memory's not what it used to be."

"I told you he wouldn't remember," said Martin sadly.

"Oh, gee!" said Henry. "I had on my new straw hat, too."

"Well, no wonder!" said the Colonel reproachfully. "How was I to know you without your hat? I've shook thousands of boys' hands since last summer. Had your breakfasts?"

"No, sir, and we've been up since four."

"Come along, then, we'll see what we can do for that."

Ardeth had an awful pang of fear. This was a man's affair and they were going off without her! She gave a little involuntary gasp of disappointment, and Martin turned around and remembered her.

"This is Ardeth," he said politely. "We call her Wienerwursts because of her hair. She's never had the pleasure of shaking your hand."

"Petticoats, eh?" said the Colonel.

"She's all right," said Henry loyally. "She has a pony and she knows how to ride it."

"That's different then. Shake hands, my girl."

Ardeth felt her hand being gripped hard by the very hand which had slain so many buffaloes. In a daze of delight, she followed along to the dining-tent.

Buffalo Bill ranged them along one of the wooden benches and banged on the bare wooden table for attention.

"Ham and eggs!" he shouted. "For Buffalo Bill and guests!"

The cooks ran about with a new burst of speed. "Coming up, Colonel! Pronto!" they cried.

Outside the tent a group of less fortunate townsboys formed a silent semicircle to watch Ardeth and the new minister's boys eating breakfast with Buffalo Bill.

In a few moments they were all talking like old friends, and Martin and Henry were telling Colonel Cody how they meant to be Indian fighters, too, as soon as they could get a horse, but how horses never seemed to go along with the Presbyterian manse in any pastorate they'd ever occupied; and Ardeth was describing her pony so that even she herself was surprised to discover how much more he sounded like a fleet Indian hunter than a fat Shetland pony who never trotted if he could in any way avoid it. As for the food, ham and eggs and buckwheat cakes had never tasted better. The plates might be thick and greasy, and the service not of the best or cleanest, but this was the meal of a lifetime!

Dr. Howard had left the house early that morning before his little daughter Ardeth was down for breakfast; but, busy as he was, Dr. Howard always tried, on circus day, to take time off at ten o'clock to see the parade with Ardeth.

"Bring her down in plenty of time, Jenny," he said as he was leaving, "and I will meet you at the corner of Main Street and Third. Be sure to have her nice and clean, and her curls well brushed."

Dr. Howard was a neat man himself, of medium height, with light-colored hair and mustache, and kind blue eyes. He was noted for his silence. "It's deeds, not words with Dr. Howard," the townspeople used to say, and wherever he went they had a smiling greeting for the doctor. Often he had to ride far into the surrounding hills to take care of sick people, and it always troubled him to think that his busy life was keeping him so much from the society of his motherless daughter. So this morning he looked forward with particular zest to seeing the *Wild West* parade in Ardeth's company.

At a quarter to ten he closed his office and went out to Main Street, where people were already lining the sidewalks to be sure of a good view of the parade. The doctor glanced up and down the street, looking for a starched pink chambray and brown curls, but he was sorry to see that Jenny and Ardeth had not yet made their appearance. As he waited on the corner of Main and Third he saw a tall, angular man, whom he knew to be his new neighbor, the Presbyterian minister, elbowing his way toward him through the crowd.

"Dr. Howard?" asked Mr. Dawlish, a bit anxiously, the doctor thought.

"Yes. Mr. Dawlish? I'm glad to meet you. Should have met you before, sir. Our children, I believe—"

"That's just it," said the minister, wiping his forehead with his handkerchief. "You don't happen to have seen my boys this morning, Dr. Howard?"

"Why, no—I—"

"They didn't come in for breakfast!" said the minister. "My boys get around a good deal, Dr. Howard, and I don't worry about them. But when they miss a meal, that's serious. I know then that something is wrong."

"Ardeth will be here at any moment," said the doctor. "Probably she can throw some light on the situation."

"That's another thing, Doctor," said Mr. Dawlish anxiously. "My wife inquired at your house—and—your daughter seems to be missing, too."

"*Ardeth missing?*" Dr. Howard was visibly shaken.

While the two men had been talking, the parade had been approaching from the direction of the railway station, and now, when they tried to cross the street to search for their lost children, they suddenly found their way blocked by a cowboy band and a troupe of feathered redskins.

"Oh, this is serious!" cried poor Dr. Howard. "When did Ardeth ever miss a circus parade?"

"There is the possibility, of course," said Mr. Dawlish, "that they may be following along at the rear of the parade. I have known such things to happen. Perhaps it is best that we stay here until it has passed by."

Just then Miss Emily Skip, of the Ladies' Aid, discovered Mr. Dawlish. At first she had a moment of horror at the idea of the new minister coming without his hat to see a *Wild West* show parade, when she herself had only happened by because of an errand which she had to do. She was not surprised at the doctor, of course, for he was always doing shocking things. Then she remembered Mr. Dawlish's boys, and her thin face crinkled into a tender smile.

"Ah, you are here with the dear little boys, Reverend Dawlish!" she cried. "And how are they enjoying the great, big, noisy parade? Not frightened, I hope?"

As there was no reply from the dear little boys among the crowd of children along the curb, Miss Skip took a hasty glance at the passing parade. The cowboy band was going *crash! bam! bam!* and there rode the famous Colonel Cody heading the best horsemen of his troupe. Cowboys were waving their lassos, Indians were uttering war whoops, horses were prancing and there was the old Deadwood coach just rumbling by. Looking out of the Deadwood coach, waving and yelling like the Indians, and twice as dirty, were the minister's little boys and the doctor's Ardeth!

"Hi, Pop, look at us!" yelled Henry.

Mr. Dawlish turned away with a sigh. He wiped his forehead and said apologetically to Miss Skip: "Boys will be boys —er—boys will be—*et cetera, et cetera.*"

Miss Skip hurried down the street, gasping with horror and trying to pretend she had not seen what she had seen. But Dr. Howard was the most shocked of all. That uncombed and unstarched apparition which had grinned at him from the window of the Deadwood coach, surely that wasn't Ardeth!

"No," said the Reverend Mr. Dawlish, his eyes twinkling as if he had read the doctor's thoughts. "Not Ardeth, that was 'Wienerwursts.'"

Ardeth and the minister's boys went to their respective beds that afternoon, instead of to the *Wild West* show, but no one minded very much, for they had ridden in the *Wild West* parade and breakfasted with Colonel Cody!

Barnum's First Circus

LAURA BENÉT

Phineas," remarked his father, pushing back his coffee cup and carefully wiping the ends of his walrus mustache, "you can tend store for me mebbe two or three days. The mare's going to take your mother and me to the county seat." He looked across the table at his thirteen-year-old son with decision.

Phineas Taylor Barnum, a stocky, broad-shouldered lad bursting with vitality, stopped munching a doughnut, and his eyes danced. This piece of news was too good to be true. He had often helped his father in the store, but to have it in charge . . . that would be wonderful!

"Yes, sir," he answered, respectfully.

His father went briskly on with the tale of his instructions. "If Noah Totten's drinking, don't give him credit. And don't give the Widow Sweeney any, neither. Cash in hand is the rule, unless circumstances is a mite unusual. Seeing apples is good this year, you can take two or three barrels in exchange for groceries. But, remember, business is likely to be brisk and you're to tend to your job and not talk your head off. You've got a good head on your shoulders when you choose to use it. That's all. And don't make me use that strap hanging up in the barn when I come back Saturday." His keen eyes twinkled slightly.

Having delivered this ultimatum, Barnum Senior, citizen of the town of Bethel, Connecticut, went to "hitch up." Barnum Junior, rejoicing in his unexpected freedom from school, put on his hat and took his way to his father's small corner store that was the town's greatest resource.

The day being October and a chill wind blowing, he began his business day by doing what his father would have said was needless extravagance. He started a fire in the rusty iron stove in the center of the store. The fire, made out of shavings, old boxes, and good hard cordwood, had not been going fifteen minutes before Phineas's first customer arrived.

It *was* the Widow Sweeney, shawled and bonneted, peering out of near-sighted, pinkish-rimmed eyes that were much like a rabbit's. She slammed the store door behind her so that everything on the shelves rattled, and delighted by the good fire, crept near it, untying her bonnet strings.

"Well, if it ain't Barnum's boy!" she ejaculated in a pleased tone. The son should be much easier to deal with than the father.

"Now, I want you," she continued, consulting a list, "to tie up a pound of white sugar and a passel of apples and raisins and two pounds of coffee and a pound of rice and a pint of sorghum molasses."

Young Barnum went to the shelves and began weighing out the various articles, to which the Widow Sweeney kept adding other items. At last everything was ready. In his pleasantest tone, he stated: "One dollar, if you please, Missus Sweeney."

The Widow started back. "No sass from you, Phineas Barnum. This is on credit today. I'm a poor woman and I pay up my bills, all at once, twice a year."

"Pa said 'no credit'—that I was to take cash only," answered Pa's representative. "I'm sorry, but you've got a long credit column already, Missus Sweeney."

Finding her first method of bluster did not work, the Widow began to wheedle. "Now, you're a good boy and not raised for impudence. Haven't I got the nicest little calf only two weeks old that I was calculating on giving your Pa in payment, if he'd continue my credit a while?"

"Is it an all right calf?" asked the youthful storekeeper bluntly.

"Of course, it's all right. It's as pretty as can be. But it's got a curious failing—an extra eye."

"Oh!" Joy gleamed in Phineas's own eyes. If he could only get hold of that calf for purposes of his own! "Pa's been wanting a calf," he answered. "Is it a bull?"

"No, a heifer."

"Well, marm—" He hesitated, the thought of the ready strap at the back of his mind, but decided he'd have to take a chance. "If you'll let me stop around tonight and see it when I close up store, I can let you have these things now."

The delighted Widow assented, warmed herself thoroughly at the stove and then went on her way. Meanwhile, Phineas Barnum resolved inwardly to "show off" that three-eyed calf behind their barn at a penny a peep—or maybe he'd make it two cents for a look. What a find for the show he was planning!

His next customer was a red-headed boy, younger than himself, who painfully lugged in two pecks of apples to be exchanged for potatoes. As he set the half-bushel basket down with a thump, a snake glided across the uneven, splintered floor toward the heat.

"Hi, help me get him, Phin! He musta got out of my pocket!" screeched Hiram Fletcher. Young Barnum recaptured the snake in a wink, stowing him in a small and dark box.

"Can you do tricks with him?" he inquired interestedly.

"Only caught him yesterday, so how'm I to know?" said Hiram, surprised by the idea.

"Bring him around to my house Saturday afternoon. Meet me behind the barn. We'll have a circus," said Phineas in an excited whisper. He saw three farmers entering, bent on leisurely purchases and conversation. "There's lots of things I can tell you, but I've got to tend store now."

Hiram chuckled. "I'll see you later and I'll get Rafe and George and Buckle Ewing, too."

Farmers were apt to stay indefinitely on such a raw day. Phineas prepared for them by fetching out a couple of rickety wooden stools (the third could perch on the molasses barrel) and mending the fire. He brought out a jug of new cider.

"Hey, Phineas," said the first farmer, Ezra Drean, a hard-bitten Yankee with rugged features and a long jaw. "Give me a plug of chewing tobacco."

The busy storekeeper cut it and was paid. "One nickel more," he requested briskly.

Ezra dumped his weather-beaten purse out on the counter for inspection. Not a cent was in it.

"I'll give you a hopping bean instead, boy!" he offered. "I know you like tricks."

"But does it really hop? Lemme see for sure."

Ezra winked at the other men and produced a small brown object from his pocket. Placing it on the bottom of a broken cracker box, he carried it to the stove. Yes, the heat caused it to skip about here and there on the piece of board. The dance was uncanny. The farmers stood and watched interestedly.

"Ain't seen a contraption like that in a month of Sundays," remarked the oldest of the three, Mose Painter.

Phineas put it carefully into his pocket.

"Thank you kindly," he capitulated, and the bean owner

joined his friends at the fire. The other two farmers, whom
Barnum's son knew to be prosperous, would buy later and pay
good greenbacks. They didn't need to bargain, save as a pas-
time.

Phineas returned to ladle out brown sugar for Eliza
Streeter.

"Look out for that sugar, now," said the stout woman,
tartly. "You ain't giving me good measure, pressed down and
running over, as the Scripture says. Don't you be skimping!"

The boy nodded amiably and overweighed the brown
sugar, though he knew what his father would have said.
The sugar, damp from recent wet weather, packed down easily.

As he waited on children, giggling schoolgirls, shrewd New
England matrons (for the store had filled up), Phineas
caught snatches of conversation from the group of farmers.

"Just try walking easy by that mill, come twilight, and
you'll hear a voice, a high, queer voice, like a spirit's," was
one statement.

"I swan. I didn't know that the old mill was haunted."

"Well, 'tis, and Steve Carter's lost his watch chain and
swears he had it when he was going by there, week or so
ago."

"Time someone got to the bottom of this," said Mose
Painter.

Then they began discussing Simon Pearce's affairs. "That
dog of his ran through town the other day looking mighty
suspicious. It might be mad and folks should look out for it."

The very same evening, Phineas, who had been to see
Widow Sweeney's three-eyed calf and agreed on a transfer,
took a walk past the old Franklin mill on the village outskirts.
He didn't believe what the men at the store had said, and
anyway, he was more curious than afraid. In the moonlight
the stone mill looked as peaceful as the stream that flowed
beside it. Suddenly, from an upper window of the mill came
easy, conversational tones.

"Good boy," uttered a clipped, mocking voice, and then a dark shadow flew past him. Something with straw clinging to it jingled at his feet. Squatting on a stone, Phineas drew from his pocket a bit of bread and a cheese rind he kept for just such emergencies. The shadow drew nearer and perched on his finger. It was a raven!

"Good night," it said, "good night, good night. Have no fear, no fear."

Adroitly, Phineas caught it, slipped it into a bag he had brought, and picked up the object on the ground. It was nothing less than Steve Carter's gold watch chain! What a surprise Steve would have on Saturday!

The raven would be a great addition to the sideshow for which Phineas could not yet persuade Amos Tutt, the man with the longest beard in the village, to be the Bearded Giant. But this raven was a find and he could teach it to talk in no time. It must have flown over from some other township where someone else had begun its education. He might rent a skull for it to perch on, if there was anyone about who had one handy. There was never going to be another exhibition like this one he planned. No, sir!

Next morning Phineas had Hiram, and George, his brother and side-partner, take a brisk turn about Bethel. One went east, one west, until they covered the whole town. In their hands they carried a pile of hand-printed advertisements that were stuck under front doors or pushed at anyone the boys happened to meet.

After three long days of storekeeping, Phineas had collected a goodly sum in his father's till as well as half-a-dozen barrels of fall pippins. Now it was Saturday noon. His father was still away, but he'd done his level best, and at three o'clock he planned to close up the store until evening.

"Barnum's Saturday Show" was opening at four o'clock for a nickel admission and a penny apiece extra for special sideshows. Of course it couldn't begin until Phineas appeared. The crowd that gathered at the back of the Barnums' barn at four o'clock that day was enormous. At a rude turnstile made of two crossed laths stood Barnum's boy himself, hair tousled, face red with excitement.

"This way, ladies and gentlemen," he shouted, "to see the Three-Eyed Calf, the only specimen of its kind in captivity. Meet Jupiter, the Domestic Snake that snuggles up to you like an infant! See the Magic Bean worked by Unseen Force, and Lupo the Raven, that talks and brings forth gold. Last chance, cash and tickets!"

"That boy of Barnum's has a gift of gab," said the tired mother of two fretting children. "First-rate showman! He'll make money or I miss my guess."

Farmers, curious to see, were driving up in carts and buggies, with children between their knees. Big boys were stamping in, leading younger brothers and sisters by the hand.

"This way, this way, to the Calf. Put your money on the Three-Eyed Calf," called one of Barnum's assistants, plaintively.

He was instantly corrected by his chief. "Say a lot more, Hi, about its unusual points—like this: 'The One and Only Calf in Captivity That Has an Extra Eye,'" shouted Phineas.

Meantime, a fearless brother, younger than Phineas, was riding Zeke, the Runaway Colt, around a chalked ring, sticking on its back despite frantic kickings and plungings. This feature, the only ten-cent one, was marvelously popular. When Bethel's crop of dimes had been taken in, the raven was produced.

"Step up here," announced the showman to late comers, "plenty of room to stand. Step up!" Then, "What do you like best, Lupo?" he asked the raven which he held up on the improvised stand.

"Gold," said Lupo in a hoarse and impressive tone.

"What next to that?"

"Chain," croaked the raven.

"And then?"

"Gold chain."

"Now. Tell the gentleman whose watch chain you took that you're sorry."

"Sor-ry," croaked the ready disciple, and Steve Carter, eyes popping, was beckoned forward to receive his missing watch chain.

"I *swan*," was all he could say.

As a final feature, the hopping bean began gamboling briskly on a table. Young Phineas had learned exactly how much heat to give it from his warm, perspiring palm.

Homemade doughnuts and cider were being circulated to the still admiring crowd when hoofs were heard approaching briskly, and a tired man came into view on the far side of the barn. In the buggy were visible the substantial shoulders of Pa Barnum, his wife by his side.

Barnum Senior's astonishment when he saw the gathering on the lot back of his barn was followed by a grim expression about the jaw. That fool boy of his, who was so keen on freaks and shows, had gone and closed up the store (yes, it was shut and silent when he passed it) and lost the late Saturday afternoon trade. He'd show him! He could not help being perked up over his son's talents, but he'd have to teach him a lesson for all that.

"Phineas," he called in tones to wake the dead, "you come here and stop this fooling."

Some little distance away, he seemed to see a familiar form, to hear a familiar voice. "Calf," it was saying.

Calf! Was it possible there was a new heifer? Excitedly, Barnum stopped the buggy, threw the reins to his wife, got out and stamped over to the circus enclosure.

"Nickel, please, Mister Barnum," requested the gatekeeper. Inwardly raging, Barnum paid it and continued his search.

"Excuse me, folks," he kept saying until suddenly, in a pen near him, he saw one of the finest little heifer calves. It was sound in wind and limb, the only defect being a curious third eye immediately over the regular one on the left side.

"Where on earth did Phineas . . . ?"

Then father and son met face to face. Young Barnum's countenance was as bland as cream. "Hey, Pa," he said. "See the calf you got from the Widow Sweeney."

"How much did you have to give for it?" roared his father.

"Not a penny. It was a present in payment."

"Well—and what do you have to say about closing the store and losing my Saturday afternoon trade?"

"I was going to reopen this evening," stated Phineas confidently, "and what I've taken in on entrances will make up for any loss. I've got a good sight of money in here, Pa, and it's all yours!" He gleefully rattled the contents of a tin can.

Parent looked at son with sudden added respect.

"You've not cheated anyone to get hold of these critters?" Barnum Senior indicated in one sweeping gesture, the calf, the raven, the snake, and the colt. "I nearly stepped on that blamed snake," he exploded as it wiggled near his boots.

"No, Pa, I didn't cheat. When folks come in to celebrate, I like to show them a thing or two," Phineas confessed. "I only quit the store an hour or so."

His father scratched his head. "I always took it you had smartness in you," was his laconic comment.

Young Barnum looked triumphantly around. The crowd was scattering. His father had made up with him and gone peering into this box and that pen to see what else he could see.

But, somehow, the barn lot wasn't quite large enough. Some day there must be a big white tent pegged down at the corners, or—maybe—a hall. In his imagination such a hall swelled and grew bigger until he had it peopled with weird shapes. He'd like a family of dwarfs—a Negro mummy—a giant—and a voice that would fill space with its ringing music and make echoes come out of the air. Some day he'd have that, too!

Doctor Dolittle's Circus

HUGH LOFTING

The circus had moved on to a town called Bridgeton, a large manufacturing center, where good business was expected by Blossom. The animals and clowns and bareback riders and the rest had made their usual procession through the streets; big bills were posted all over the place, and when the enclosure was opened to the public, great throngs of people had crowded up to the gates. It looked like one of the best weeks the circus had ever known.

At two o'clock the show at the big tent (for which an extra sixpence was charged) was to begin. Outside the entrance a large sign was set up showing the program: "Mademoiselle Firefly, the Bareback Rider; the Pinto Brothers, Daring Trapeze Artists; Hercules, the Strongest Man on Earth; Hop, the Side-Splitting Clown, and His Comedy Wonder-Dog, Swizzle; Jojo, the Dancing Elephant," and (in large letters) "NINO, the World-Famous Talking Horse."

Now this Nino was just an ordinary, cream-colored cob who had been trained to answer signals. Blossom had bought him from a Frenchman; and with him he had bought the secret of his so-called talking. In his act he didn't talk at all, really. All he did was to stamp his hoof or wag his head a certain number of times to give answers to the questions Blossom asked him in the ring.

"How many do three and four make, Nino?" Blossom would say. Then Nino would stamp the floor seven times. And if the answer was *yes*, he would nod his head up and down, and if it was *no*, he would shake it from side to side. Of course, he didn't know what was being asked of him at all, as a matter of fact. And the way he knew what answers to give was from the signals that Blossom made to him secretly. When he wanted Nino to say *yes*, the ringmaster would scratch his left ear; when he wanted him to answer *no*, he would fold his arms, and so on. The secret of all these signals Blossom kept jealously to himself. But, of course, the Doctor knew all about them because Nino had told him how the whole performance was carried on.

Now, in advertising the circus, Blossom always put Nino, the World-Famous Talking Horse, before all the other turns in importance. It was a popular performance and the children loved shouting questions down to the little plump cob and seeing him answer with his feet or his head.

Well, on the circus's first day in Bridgeton, a little before the show in the big tent was to begin, the Doctor and the ringmaster were in the clown's dressing-room talking. Suddenly in rushed the head stableman in a great state of excitement.

"Mr. Blossom," he cried, "Nino's sick! Layin' in 'is stall with 'is eyes closed. The show's due to begin in fifteen minutes and I can't do nothing with 'im—can't even get 'im on 'is feet."

With a hearty curse Blossom rushed out and tore away in the direction of the stables, while the Doctor followed him on the run.

When they got to Nino's stall Blossom and the Doctor found the horse in a bad state. His breathing was fast and heavy. With difficulty he was made to stand up on his feet, but for walking even a few steps he seemed far too shaky and weak.

"Darn the luck!" muttered the manager. "If he can't perform it will queer the whole week's showing. We've posted him as the star turn. The crowd will want to know about it if they don't see him."

"You'll have to make a speech and explain," said the Doctor. "That horse has a bad fever. I doubt if he can leave his stall today."

"Good heavens, man, he'll have to!" cried Blossom. "We'll likely have the audience asking for its money back if he don't appear. We can't have any more riots like—"

At that moment a boy came up.

"Five minutes to two, Mr. Blossom. Pierce wants to know if you are all ready."

"Hang it!" said the manager. "I can't take the ring for the first turn. I must get Nino fixed up before I can come on."

"We ain't got nobody else, sir," said the boy. "Robinson 'asn't got back yet."

"Lord, what a day!" groaned the manager. "Well, the show can't open without a ringmaster, that's sure. And I can't leave Nino yet. I don't know what—"

"Excuse me, governor," said a voice behind him. And turning, Blossom looked into the crossed eyes of Matthew Mugg.

"Couldn't I take your place, boss?" said the Cat's Meat-Man. "I know your whole line of talk by heart. I could introduce the turns—same as you—and nobody know the difference."

"Well," said Blossom, looking him up and down, "you're about the scrubbiest ringmaster I ever see'd. But beggars can't be choosers. Come with me—quick—and I'll give you these clothes."

Then, while the Doctor turned his attention to Nino, Blossom and Matthew made off on the run for the dressing-rooms.

There, with the aid of Theodosia (who put a large swift pleat in Blossom's riding breeches) and a little rouge and a false mustache from the clown's make-up box, Mr. Mugg was transformed from a cat's-meat-man into a ringmaster. The ambition of his life was realized at last. And as he swaggered into the ring and looked up at the sea of faces around him, his chest swelled with dignity, while Theodosia, watching him through a slit in the tent-flap, glowed with wifely pride and prayed that the pleat in his riding breeches would hold till the show was over.

In the meantime from an examination of Nino the Doctor became certain that there was no hope of his recovering in time to perform that day. He went and got some large pills from his black bag and gave him two. Presently Blossom, now dressed in a jersey and flannel pants, joined him.

"You can't have this horse perform today, Mr. Blossom," said the Doctor, "nor for a week, probably, at least."

"Well," said the ringmaster, throwing up his hands in despair, "we're just ruined—that's all—ruined! That row up in Stowbury got into the papers, and now if we have another frost here, we're done for. And if Nino don't go on, the crowd's going to ask for their money back, sure as you're alive. He's the star turn. We might manage if we had another act to put on in his place, but I haven't a blessed thing for an extra. And it was a short program, anyhow. We're ruined. Darn it, I never saw such a run of rotten luck!"

Poor Blossom seemed genuinely crestfallen. While the Doctor looked at him thoughtfully, a horse in the stall next to Nino's neighed softly. It was Beppo, the veteran wagon horse. A smile came into the Doctor's face.

"Look here, Mr. Blossom," said he quietly, "I think I can help you out of this trouble, but if I do you've got to promise me a few things. I know a good deal more about animals than you suppose I do. I've given up the best part of my life to studying them. You advertised that Nino understood you and could answer any questions you put to him. You and I know that's not so, don't we? The trick was done by a system of signals. But it took the public in. Now I'm going to tell you a secret of my own which I don't boast about because nobody would believe me if I did. I can talk to horses in their own language and understand them when they talk back to me."

Blossom was staring down moodily at the floor while the Doctor spoke. But at the last words he gazed up at John Dolittle frowning.

"Are you crazy?" he said, "or didn't I hear straight? Talk to animals in their own language! Look 'ere: I've been in the show business thirty-seven years, knocked around with animals ever since I was a nipper. And I know there ain't no such thing as a man talking with a horse in horse language. You got a cheek to tell me a yarn like that—me, Alexander Blossom!"

"I am not telling you a yarn," said the Doctor quietly. "I am telling you the truth. But I can see that you will not believe me till I prove it to you."

"You bet I won't," sneered Blossom.

"Well, there are five horses in this stable, aren't there?" asked the Doctor. "And none of them can see me here where I stand, can they? Now if you will ask me to put some question to any one of them I will endeavor to give you his answer."

"Oh, you're crazy!" said Blossom. "I ain't got time to fool with you."

"All right," said the Doctor. "My intention was to help, as I told you. But, of course, if you don't want my assistance, then that ends the matter."

He shrugged his shoulders and turned away. The noise of clapping sounded from the big tent.

"Ask Beppo," said Blossom, "what's the number of the stall he's in."

Beppo's was the second from the end. On his door was marked a large "2" in white paint.

"Do you wish to have him tell me the answer in horse

language," asked the Doctor, "or shall I have him tap the number?"

"Have him tap the partition with his foot, Professor," sneered Blossom. "I don't know no horse grammar; and I couldn't tell, t'other way, whether you was faking or not."

"Very good," said the Doctor. And from where he stood, quite invisible to Beppo, he made some snuffly breathing noises—rather as though he had a cold in his head. Immediately two taps sounded from stall No. 2.

Blossom's eyebrows went up in surprise. But almost immediately he shrugged his shoulders.

"Pshaw! Could easily 'ave been an accident. Maybe he just fell against the partition. Ask 'im—er—ask 'im 'ow many buttons I 'ave on my waistcoat—the one your cross-eyed assistant is wearing in the ring now."

"All right," said the Doctor. And he made some more snuffly noises, ending with a gentle whinny.

But this time, unintentionally, he did not include Beppo's name in his message. Now all the five horses in that stable knew Blossom's waistcoat very well, of course. And each one thought the question was being asked of him. Suddenly from every stall six sharp raps rang out, and even poor Nino, lying in the straw with his eyes closed, stretched out a hind leg and weakly kicked his door six times. Mr. Blossom's eyes looked as though they were going to pop out of his head.

"Now," said the Doctor smiling, "in case you should think that was accidental too, I will ask Beppo to pull down the rag you see there hanging on his partition and to throw it up in the air."

In response to a few more words of horse language, the rag, whose end hung over the top of the partition, suddenly disappeared. The Doctor had not moved. Blossom ran down the stable to look inside stall No. 2. There he found the aged wagon horse tossing the rag up in the air and catching it— rather like a schoolgirl playing with a handkerchief.

"Now do you believe me?" asked the Doctor.

"Believe you!" cried Blossom. "I believe you're the Devil's younger brother. Just the same, you're the man I want, all right. Come on down to the dressing-room and let's put some togs on you."

"Just a minute," said the Doctor. "What do you mean to do?"

"Dress you up," said Blossom, "of course. You're going to do a turn for us, ain't you? Why, you could take any cab horse and make a Nino of him. You said you was going to help me."

"Yes," answered John Dolittle slowly, "and I will—after, as I told you, you have promised me a few things. I am willing to make Beppo provide your ring with a talking horse on certain conditions. Nino's act doesn't come on till the end of the show. We have a half-hour to talk this over in."

"There's no need," cried Blossom, all excited. "I'll promise you any bloomin' thing. Why, if you can talk animals' language we'll make a fortune in a season! Lor' bless us! I never believed you could do it. You ought to 'ave joined the show business years ago. You'd 'ave bin a rich man by now—instead of a broken-down country doctor. Come on over and we'll pick you out some nifty togs. Can't go in them baggy trousers; people 'ud think you'd never bin on a horse in your life."

Blossom and the Doctor left the stable and made their way across to the dressing-rooms where, out of some of the well-traveled trunks, the ringmaster began pulling costume after costume and piling them on the floor. While he was going through the gaudy clothes the Doctor laid down the conditions under which he would give the performance.

"Now, Mr. Blossom," said he, "ever since I have been with your concern I have noticed certain things that were distasteful to my ideas of honest business and the humanitarian treatment of animals. Some of these I have brought to your attention and in almost all cases you refused to listen to me."

"Why, Doctor," said Mr. Blossom, yanking a pair of red Persian trousers out of a trunk, "how can you say such a thing? Didn't I get rid of Brown and Fatima because you objected to 'em?"

"You parted with them because you had to," said the Doctor, "not to oblige me. I have felt very uneasy about being part of a show which I did not consider strictly honest. It would take a long time to go into all the details. For the present, the bargain I am going to strike with you is this: Beppo, the horse I will use for the talking act, is far too old to work. He has been in service now thirty-five years. I want him, as a reward for this help which he will give you, to be pensioned off for the remainder of his days, made comfortable and given the kind of life he likes."

"I agree. Now how would this do?"

Blossom held up a cavalier's jerkin against the Doctor's chest. "No—too small. You ain't very high from the ground, but you're full-sized around the middle, all right."

"The other thing I want you to do," the Doctor went on, as Blossom turned back to the trunk for another costume, "is to put your menagerie in proper order. The cages are not cleaned often enough; some of the animals have not sufficient space for their needs, and many of them never get the kinds of food they like best."

"All right, Doc, we'll do anything in reason. I'll let you draw up a set of rules for the menagerie-keeper and you can see that he toes the line. 'Ow would you like to be a Western cowboy?"

"I wouldn't," said the Doctor. "They are inconsiderate of their cattle. And I don't approve of that silly business of flapping a hat in a horse's eyes to make him buck. Then, for the rest, I shall from time to time expect you to make many minor reforms for the animals' comfort. I shall expect you to treat my suggestions reasonably and co-operate with me for their welfare. What do you say?"

"I say it's a go, Doc," said Blossom. "We ain't begun yet. If

you stay with my outfit for a year—with your gift of talking
to animals—why!—I'll make every other circus look like a
twopenny peepshow. Oh my! 'ere's the very thing—a cavalry
uniform—Twenty-first Hussars. Just your size. Medals and
all! Suits your complexion, too."

This time Blossom held a bright-scarlet tunic over the Doctor's bosom and beamed on him with delight.

"Ever seen anything so nifty!" he chuckled. "My word! I
tell you—we'll make this town sit up! Could you get these
things on your feet?"

"Oh, I dare say," said the Doctor, taking a gaudy pair of
military riding boots from the ringmaster and sitting down
to unlace his own. At that moment the door opened and a
stable boy came in.

"Joe, you're just in time," said Blossom. "Run over to the
stables and give Beppo a rub-down with a currycomb. 'E's
going to do an act."

"*Beppo!*" cried the boy incredulously.

"That's what I said, block-'ead!" shouted Blossom. "And
put the green 'alter on 'im with the white rosettes—and braid
'is tail with a red ribbon. 'Op about it!"

As the lad disappeared, the clown with Swizzle entered
for a short rest between acts. The Doctor, in smart regimen-
tal breeches and top boots, was now buttoning up the scarlet
tunic about his chin.

" 'Ow's my cross-eyed understudy doing?" asked Blossom.

"Governor, he's a wonder!" said Hop sinking into a chair.
"A born ringmaster. You never heard such a voice. He's got
a gift of gab, all right. Ready with a joke if anybody slips;
cracking quips with the audience—I tell you, governor,
you've got to look to your laurels if you leave him with the
ladies for long. Who's the military gentleman? My hat, it's
the Doctor! What's he going to do?"

At this moment another lad ran in.

"Only ten minutes before the last act goes on, Mr. Blossom," he cried.

"All right," said Blossom. "We can do it. Here's your sword-belt, Doctor. How's the crowd, Frank?"

"Great!" said the boy. "Pleased as Punch! They brought the whole grammar school down at the last minute. And the Soldiers' and Sailors' Home is coming tonight. People standing two-deep in the aisles. It's the biggest business we've played to this year."

Tremendous excitement now prevailed behind the scenes in Blossom's "Mammouth Circus." As the clown, Hop, opened the dressing-room door to go back into the ring, mingled cheers and hand-clapping, the noise of the big audience's applause, reached the ears of John Dolittle and the manager.

"Listen, 'Op," said Blossom, "pass the word to Mugg as you go back in that Nino is going to play anyway—in substitute—and the Doc 'ere is doing the part of the trainer. Mugg can give 'em the introduction patter just the same. Tell 'im to lay it on thick. It's going to be the greatest little turn we ever showed—better than Nino at 'is best."

"All right, governor," said the clown, grinning through his paint. "But I wish you had picked a better-looking horse."

At the last moment one of the Doctor's shoulder straps was found to be loose. Only two minutes now remained before his act was due. Someone flew off and found Theodosia and with frantic haste she put it right with a needle and thread. Then, complete in his gay and wonderful uniform, the Doctor ran out of the dressing-room to join his partner, Beppo, whose bridle was being held at the entrance to the big tent by the boy, Frank.

Poor Beppo did not look nearly as smart as the Doctor. Years of neglect and haphazard grooming could not be remedied by one currycombing. His coat was long and dingy-looking, his mane straggly and unkempt. In spite of the smart green-and-white headstall and the red ribbon in his plaited tail, he looked what he was: an old, old servant who had done his work faithfully for many, many years and got little credit or thanks for it.

"Oh, I say, Beppo!" the Doctor murmured in his ear as he took the bridle from Frank. "Anyone would think you were going to a funeral. Brace up! Draw your head back, high. That's it. Now blow out your nostrils. Ah, much better!"

"You know, Doctor," said Beppo, "you mightn't believe it, but I come of a very good family. My mother used to trace her pedigree way back to the battle-charger that Julius Caesar used—the one he always rode when he reviewed the Praetorian Guard. My mother was very proud of it. She took first prizes, she did. But when the heavy battle-chargers went out of fashion, all the big military horses got put to draft work. That's how we came down in the world. Oughtn't we to rehearse this act a bit first? I've no idea of what I'm expected to do."

"No, we haven't time now," said John Dolittle. "We are liable to be called on any minute. But we'll manage. Just do everything I tell you—and put in any extras you think of yourself. Look out, you're drooping your head again. Remember your Roman ancestor. Chin up—that's the way. Arch your neck. Make your eyes flash. Look as though you were carrying an emperor who owned the earth. . . . Fine! That's the style! Now you look great."

Within the big canvas theater Mr. Matthew Mugg, ringmaster for a day, was still covering himself with glory, bossing "The Greatest Show on Earth" with creditable skill, and introducing the performers with much oratory and unusual grammar. He was having the time of his life and making the most of it.

In between the turns of the Pinto Brothers and the Strong Man, he saw Hop return into the ring and recommence his antics which always so delighted the children. As the clown did a somersault past the ringmaster's nose, Matthew heard him whisper: "The boss is putting on another talking horse with the Doctor playing the trainer. He wants you to introduce him the same as Nino."

"Right you are," Matthew whispered back. "I've got the idea."

And when Jojo, the dancing elephant, had bowed himself out amidst a storm of applause, the ringmaster stepped to the entrance-flap and himself led forward the next, the star, turn.

For a moment old Beppo, accompanied by a short stout man in cavalry uniform, seemed a little scared to find a sea of faces staring down at him.

Motioning to the strange-looking performers to remain by the edge of the ring a moment, Matthew advanced into the center. With a lordly wave of the hand he silenced the wheezy band who were still finishing Jojo's last dance. And in the quiet that followed he looked up at the audience and filled his lungs for his last and most impressive speech.

"Ladies and gentlemen," roared Ringmaster Mugg, "we 'ave now harrived at the last and most himportant act in our long and helegant program. You 'ave all 'eard, I'm sure, of Nino—Nino, the world-famous Talking 'Orse, and his gallant owner, the dashing Cossack cavalry officer, Captain Nicholas Pufftupski. There they are, ladies and gentlemen; you see them before you in the flesh. Kings and queens have traveled miles to witness their act. Only two months ago, when we were playing in Monte Carlo, we 'ad to turn away the Prime Minister of England because we 'adn't got a seat for 'im in the 'ouse.

"Nino, ladies and gentlemen, is very old. He came originally from the back steppes of Siberia. His present owner, Major Pufftupski, bought 'im from the wandering Tartar tribes. Since then 'e 'as been through fifteen wars—which accounts for his wore-out appearance. This is the self-same 'orse that Colonel Pufftupski rode when, single 'anded, 'e drove Napoleon out of Moscow and saved Russia from fallin' under the hiron 'eel of Bonaparte. And the center one of them three medals you see 'anging on the Brigadier's chest is the one the Czar gave 'im as a reward for 'is brave hact."

"Oh, stop this nonsense, Matthew," whispered the Doctor coming up to him, dreadfully embarrassed. "There's no need to . . ."

But the eloquent ringmaster hurried on with thunderous voice: "So much, ladies and gentlemen, for the military career of this remarkable 'orse and 'is brave owner. General Pufftupski is a modest man and he forbids me to tell you about 'is other medals that was given 'im by the King of Sweden and the Empress of China. I now pass on to the hextraordinary hintelligence of the animal you see before you. On 'is way back from chasing Napoleon out of Russia, Count Pufftupski was took prisoner—and 'is 'orse, the famous Nino, with 'im. During their himprisonment they became very hintimate. So much so that at the end of the two years while they was captives of the French, Nino and 'is owner could talk to one another freely—the same as you and I might do. If you don't believe what I say you can prove it for yourselves. All you 'ave to do is to ask any question of Nino through his owner and it will be answered—if it 'as an answer. The Field Marshal talks all languages except Japanese. If any Japanese ladies or gentlemen in the audience wants to ask questions they'll 'ave to turn 'em into some other language first. Marshal Pufftupski will open 'is performance with this marvelous 'orse with a few tricks just to show you what they can do. Ladies and gentlemen, I 'ave great pleasure in introducing to you the Archduke Nicholas Pufftupski, Commander-in-Chief of the Russian Army, and 'is battle-charger, the one and only, world-famous, NINO."

As the band played a few opening chords the Doctor and Beppo stepped forward to the center of the ring and bowed. A tremendous burst of applause came from the people.

It was a strange performance, the only one of its kind ever given to a circus audience. The Doctor, when he was entering the ring, had no definite idea of what he was going to do— neither had Beppo. But the old, old veteran knew that the performance was going to win him comfort and freedom from work for the rest of his days. Every once in a while during the course of the act he would forget his noble ancestry and slump back into his usual weary, worn-out appearance. But on the whole, as Hop said afterward, he made a much better looking show horse than anyone had expected; and so far as the audience was concerned, his success surpassed anything Blossom had ever exhibited.

After doing a few tricks Colonel Pufftupski turned to the people and offered (in remarkably good English) to make the horse do anything they asked.

Immediately a little boy in the front row cried out: "Tell him to come over here and take my hat off."

The Doctor made a sign or two and Beppo went straight to the boy, lifted the cap from his head and put it into his hand. Then numberless questions were shouted by the audience, and to every one Beppo gave an answer—sometimes by tapping the floor, sometimes by shaking his head, and sometimes by word of mouth which the Doctor translated. The people enjoyed it so much that Blossom, watching through a slit outside, thought they'd never be done. And when at last the gallant Pufftupski led his horse out of the ring, the audience clapped and cheered and called to him again and again to come back and receive their applause.

The news of the wonderful success of the circus's first performance in Bridgeton, mostly brought about by the marvelous Talking Horse, quickly spread through the town. And long before the evening show was due, people were lined up outside the big tent, four deep, waiting patiently to make sure of seats; while the rest of the enclosure and all the sideshows were packed and thronged so tight that you could hardly move through the crowds.

Oscar at the Circus

MABEL NEIKIRK

There is one thing about this circus that I don't like," said Oscar, the trained seal.

"Why," said Mr. Zabriski, his trainer, "I thought you enjoyed every bit of your act."

"Oh, the tricks are all right," Oscar replied, "but I never get a chance to dress up. You spend a good half-hour before every performance trimming yourself like a Christmas tree, but what do I put on? Absolutely nothing! You wear your shiny black boots and your white breeches and your pink coat with all the gold braid and medals, and now you have that officer's cap with the visor. I must say you surely do look elegant. But can I put on a policeman's suit or even a cowboy outfit? No! I must wear my same old fur skin day in and day out. It's tiresome, I tell you!"

"But Oscar, be sensible," argued Mr. Zabriski. "Answer

me. Could you do all those fancy dives dressed as a cowboy or a policeman?"

"Of course I couldn't," Oscar scolded. "But just the same, I wish I could. I tell you it takes all the joy out of my life." He borrowed Mr. Zabriski's handkerchief and pretended to wipe a tear out of his eye.

"Perhaps you could wear a red bathing suit," Mr. Zabriski suggested kindly. "That would be a change. Something in stripes ought to look well. You'd like that, wouldn't you? We'll talk it over after the show. But come now. It's time for our act and we must go into the tent. Are you ready?"

Oscar really did enjoy acting. While he limbered up in his tank before a performance, Mr. Zabriski always made a short speech explaining to the audience that the tricks were really very difficult. He would frequently pick out a gentleman sitting in the front row and point to him with his short cane, saying: "Tell me, sir, can *you* balance balls on your nose?"

Usually, he'd question a young lady next. "Miss, could you climb a stepladder with a glass of iced tea on your head, and never spill a drop?" he would ask.

Everybody in the tent would laugh at those jokes, and then Mr. Zabriski would ask them to clap their hands after each trick, pointing out that Oscar always worked twice as hard when friendly people in the audience showed him that they liked his performance.

After that, Oscar would flop out of the water and the show would begin. Fancy diving, and balancing balls and iced tea weren't all that Oscar did. He played tunes on trumpets, he beat a drum, and he even pulled a little express wagon around the ring with a Teddy bear sitting on the seat pretending to drive. And as Oscar finished each trick, while the audience applauded, Mr. Zabriski patted him affectionately, and for a reward threw him a small piece of fish.

On the day that Mr. Zabriski suggested the bathing suit, Oscar performed better than ever before. He felt tremen-

dously encouraged, and during the show he made plans for
his wardrobe.

"I could walk into the ring wearing a silk bathrobe, a blue
one with a big white 'O' for Oscar sewed on the front," he
said to himself. "And when I'd throw that off, there I'd be
in my red-striped bathing suit!"

He could hardly wait until the show was over to tell Mr.
Zabriski his ideas. However, as events turned out, the seal
found no time to talk about bathing suits. He was soon much
too busy doing something else.

On the way out of the tent that afternoon, Oscar met one
of his friends, a clown.

"Hello there," called Oscar, cheerfully.

"Hello," said the clown, not at all cheerfully.

"What's the matter?" Oscar asked. "It's a good thing your
mouth is painted so that the corners turn up in a smile, for
if your face looked the way your voice sounds, you'd have
the audience crying instead of laughing."

"I *could* cry without half trying," answered the clown
gloomily. "I've just received a telephone message that we
have a nice new baby at our house—a little girl baby—and I
can't go home to see her because I must jump about in that
tent again tonight and try hard to make a lot of people laugh.
I tell you, I don't feel a bit like rolling a hoop around that
ring and acting silly! If I could only find someone to take
my place tonight."

"Yes, if you only could," said Oscar. "Why, you can!" he
added suddenly. "You *have* found someone. *I* will take your
place!"

"You couldn't," said the clown.

"I could," said Oscar.

"What would you wear?" asked the clown.

"What do you think? A clown suit, of course," said Oscar
cheerfully.

"Mine would never fit *you*," said the clown.

"Well, then, make me one! For *goodness sake*," Oscar

scolded, "don't let little difficulties discourage you so easily. Make me a crepe-paper suit."

"I suppose I could," said the clown thoughtfully.

"Of course you could," replied Oscar. "Come on. Let's go."

So they set to work, the clown cutting, sewing, and fitting, and Oscar doing his share, pasting, and standing still while the clown stuck in pins and fastened threads.

The suit was made of light-green paper with many curled ruffles that were cut and gathered like large petals. They covered Oscar's flippers, making him look exactly like a giant head of lettuce. He wore a small white false-face and a flat, red, wagon-wheel hat that resembled a slice of tomato. And when the clown had fastened the last thread, he looked at Oscar and laughed.

"You surely look fresh!" he exclaimed. "All you need is a spoonful of mayonnaise dressing and someone might try to eat you."

"No one will guess that I'm Oscar when I wear this costume," said the seal.

And he was right, for when he entered the tent that evening, he could hear people saying: "Look over there! Look at that clown! He's dressed to look like a salad! What next?"

Now, of course, Oscar wasn't used to doing clown tricks. When the audience first saw him, they laughed and clapped, but in a short time the seal noticed that they were no longer laughing at him. They were enjoying the foolishness of the other clowns, but paying no attention to the head of lettuce.

He picked up a ball and tried to balance it on his nose, but the false face was in his way, so that trick was no good. He couldn't stand on his head or roll over, for every time he tried it, he heard ripping and tearing sounds in the ruffles. So, feeling quite discouraged, he walked over to the big seal tank in the center of the stage and began walking around it, balancing himself on the edge.

"What can I do to make them laugh?" he asked himself. "I

know," he said. "I'll pretend to fall in, but save myself just in time."

He swayed toward the water, he swayed back, he swayed toward the water again and then back. People in the audience began pointing to him and laughing and clapping.

"Now I am getting somewhere at last," said the seal. And he was happy once more, because, after all, Oscar wasn't just a tiresome show-off, wanting everyone to notice him. He was an *actor*, and making the audience look at him was the most important part of his business.

But the new game didn't last very long. In a little while no one laughed any more. The people grew tired of watching the head of lettuce almost fall in and never quite do it, and they began looking at the other clowns.

"I must do something different again," Oscar worried. "This showing-off business is hard work. What can I do now? I have it! This time I'll really fall in!"

Once more he balanced on the edge of the tank. He was trying so hard to make people laugh that he thought of nothing else and he forgot that he was all dressed up in a costume made of paper. Then, *splash!* over he went into the deep tank, and the audience clapped and called: "Man overboard!" and: "Throw him a package of Life Savers!"

But while they were applauding, Oscar, down at the bottom of the tank, realized that he was in trouble; for when he hit the water the green crepe paper fell off in soggy chunks and the false-face crumpled up and floated away, too. And there he was, just a slippery seal swimming around under water, with nothing left of the beautiful costume but a few white strings clinging to his neck and flippers. He dared not come to the surface, and being used to swimming under water, it never occurred to him that the audience would expect him to bob up on top.

And while Oscar swam about under water, everyone in the tent sat with eyes glued to the pool. At first the audience thought it was a joke, but in a few minutes people began to look worried and someone called: "He didn't come up! He can't swim!"

Screams were heard and people were crying: "Save him! Save him!"

Three men came running from the back seats of the tent and a girl jumped up from her place in the front row. They raced across the ring and all jumped into the tank at once to rescue Oscar. They were all good swimmers, but naturally Oscar was better. He ducked around under water slipping through their fingers in a game of hide and seek, but at last they caught him. When they found that they had saved a seal from drowning, they were not only surprised but disgusted.

Oscar couldn't truthfully say: "Thank you for rescuing me. You've saved my life." He didn't know what to say. He just sat there on the edge of the tank feeling very foolish. Finally he remarked to the three dripping rescuers: "Hello, everybody!"

"He could swim all the time," cried the first man, "and now I'm soaking wet!"

"Just take a look at *my* new suit! Take a look at it!" the second man yelled.

"And look at my best dress!" the girl cried furiously. "I want to see the manager."

By this time the manager was on his way down the aisle; and Mr. Zabriski, seeing that something had gone wrong, was hurrying toward the stage. And at that point Oscar began to feel very unpopular. He wished that he could suddenly vanish, but he wasn't an elf and he didn't know how to disappear; so he did the next best thing. He shut his eyes, rolled over and played dead doggy.

"He's sick!" the girl exclaimed. "The poor thing! And I was scolding him."

"Is there a doctor in the house?" called the manager, while Mr. Zabriski knelt on the floor looking worried and wishing that he knew more about first aid.

There was a doctor in the circus tent and he lost no time

getting to the stage, but he was a young man and he had never been called to the bedside of a seal before. He dropped down on one knee beside Oscar, murmuring helplessly: "This is very unusual. I think that you had better consult a fish doctor."

"Can't you give him some medicine?" Mr. Zabriski begged.

"Get busy, man! Do something!" yelled the nervous manager who was used to giving orders. "Can't you tell us if he is alive? Is his heart beating?"

The doctor felt in his pocket, and drew out a little rubber-tubing telephone that is called a stethoscope. He put the tips to his ears, and began moving the metal piece across Oscar's chest. Oscar held his breath as long as he could, but finally he could hold it no longer.

"E-e-e-e-e! You tickle!" he yelled, coming to life.

"Faker!" shouted the doctor.

"He ruined my Sunday dress," scolded the girl.

"You'll pay for this!" the first man cried, scowling at the manager.

"And what about *my* suit?" roared the second man.

Mr. Zabriski saw that things didn't look very bright. "Come on, Oscar," he said gently. "We'd better go."

"Go?" shouted the manager. "Did you say 'go'?" his voice thundered through the tent. "*You're fired!* Do you understand? You don't—work here—any more! Get out of my show!"

At that the audience began to clap and Mr. Zabriski whispered sadly to Oscar: "They're *glad* we've lost our jobs." Then he walked quietly away, and the seal, with hanging head, followed him sorrowfully from the tent.

But they had no sooner reached Oscar's dressing-room than the manager came running. "Come quickly and take a bow," he cried. As Oscar and Mr. Zabriski followed the manager back to the tent, they heard a tremendous uproar.

"We want Oscar," the people were calling as they clapped and cheered. "We want Oscar!"

"They don't realize that the whole thing was an accident," whispered the manager. "They think that it was all part of the show, that you did it on purpose."

So Oscar, the doctor, the three swimmers, Mr. Zabriski, and the manager all joined hands and bowed; and *eight* more times, as they went off stage, the audience clapped them back again.

But finally when the tent had emptied, the manager said: "Let's talk business. This is the best act I've ever had. We'll do the whole thing over every night."

He told the doctor: "When you can't come, send someone else. I'll pay well."

He put money into the girl swimmer's hand. "Buy yourself a nice new dress and come back here again tomorrow night and ruin it," he said.

He put money into the men swimmers' hands. "Come back and ruin your suits, too," he said.

And then he shook hands with Mr. Zabriski, and patted Oscar on the shoulder. "*Some actor!* You're going to get a raise!" he exclaimed. "What a show! What a show!"

The Bear

RUTH MANNING-SANDERS

On a spring evening, in the orchard behind the farm where
Tom Pagett's circus was still in its winter quarters, the entire
Pagett family, together with such other circus folk as win-
tered with them, were gathered in front of the brown bear's
cage.

In the adjacent cages, the lions and tigers, having been fed
by Josef, their Spanish trainer, were settling themselves for
sleep. But the brown bear's supper—and his morning's breakfast—lay untouched on the floorboards of his cage.

The bear, whom they had christened Boxer, because of
the enormous strength of his forepaws, had been with Pagett's
for exactly a week, and all that time Tom had been putting
food before him—tempting him with every delicacy he could
think of. And all that time Boxer had eaten nothing.

Now, as the circus folk stood in a puzzled group and stared through the bars at him, Boxer, with his face so devoid of expression that it did not even express grief, sat humped against the back wall of his cage, and stared over their heads into vacancy.

"Anybody'd think we were trying to poison the animal—he's so suspicious," said Hester Pagett, Tom's wife.

"I don't like being beaten," said Tom, "but I reckon we'll just have to send him back. He's pining, that's what it is—he'll be nothing but skin and bone presently."

"That's right—send him packing," agreed Hester. "He's nasty-tempered. He'd as soon crush anybody's head in as look at 'em. And those claws! I feel queer every time you go to put food before him."

"He misses his brothers and sisters," said Josef, who had a very tender and understanding heart. "He is alone for the first time in his life—you comprehend? It would have been better, Boss, if you had bought the whole troupe."

"So I would have—didn't get the chance. Was let down over the job," explained Tom.

"Those animals—they've got poker faces," observed Ferny, the elephant-keeper. "You can't read 'em like you can pachyderms. You can always tell what a pachyderm's thinking."

"We can all do all right without a bear, anyhow," said young Jacky Pagett, who, at sixteen, had just been promoted to show the monkeys, and didn't, at the moment, "give a durn for anything but simians," as he put it.

"Pity, though," remarked a groom. "He must weigh above six hundred pounds. And the coat on him—never see such a creature!"

"But 'tisn't as if he was a horse," chimed in Dan Pagett, the boy rider. "It's horses make up the circus, ain't it, Dad?"

"All of us make up the circus," answered Tom Pagett. "But that animal's going back where he came from tomorrow."

With her small, sharp face upturned within six inches of

the bars, little Andalusa, Pagett's youngest, stood among the group of older people, and stared, as they all stared, at the bear. She looked rather a top-heavy little figure, with her mane of dark chestnut hair falling heavily over her shoulders, and her childish legs encased in a diminutive pair of jodhpurs. Her mouth was slightly open, and her lips were slightly pouting, and her yellow-brown eyes were almost as vacant-seeming as the bear's own. This was the expression she wore when she sat among the audience in the circus tent, and followed every act, and every inflection of every act, of Pagett's show. It signalized an all-out concentration on the matter in hand. As Tom Pagett had been more than once heard to remark: "There's no flies on our Lu when she pulls that face."

Well, come to that, there weren't many flies on Andalusa at any time.

One after another the older folk drifted away from the bear's cage. Hester went to prepare the family's evening meal. Ferny went back to the elephant shed, where that seven-ton-weight of petted childishness, the Queen of Sheba, who couldn't bear him out of her sight for more than a few moments, weaved restlessly at her picket and trumpeted her need of him. Josef went to telephone the knackers about a further supply of meat for his big cats, and Jacky to give the monkeys their supper; there was no question about *their* appetites, they were complaining now like a nursery full of hungry babies.

Left alone in front of the bear's cage, Andalusa became conversational.

"*Aren't* you a silly old bear?" she said derisively.

There was no response to this sally. Andalusa pressed her nose against the bars to look at Boxer, and Boxer stared over Andalusa's head into vacancy.

"Don't you want to work on our show?" queried Andalusa. "You've got to work on some show—got to. And there's none so good as ours."

Humped dejectedly against the back wall of the cage, Boxer gazed into vacancy.

"You get treated good on our show," said Andalusa persuasively. "You know that."

Boxer didn't seem to know it.

"But we can't have skinny things about," went on Andalusa. "Doesn't look well. You best make up your mind to eat."

A stale bun-loaf was lying just inside the cage. Andalusa got a stick and poked the loaf across the floorboards. "This has got currants in," she explained, prodding the bun-loaf against Boxer's haunch. "Come on, eat it!"

A queer sound that was something between a growl and a moan sounded in Boxer's throat, but he didn't look at the loaf, nor at the stick, nor at Andalusa. Nor did he move a muscle.

Andalusa pulled the stick out of the cage and threw it away. "You aren't tough enough," she remarked. "That's what's the matter with you. *I'm* tough. I don't mind where I go, or who I go with. Went to Ireland once, and wasn't sick. Might go to America tomorrow. And *I* wouldn't mope the way you do. I'd eat and eat all the way over."

"Anda-lus-a!" That was Hester calling. "Supper!"

Andalusa pushed back her hair from her face, and expressed herself finally.

"You aren't bad-looking—in your way. But you aren't tough enough."

Hester had done a big baking that day, and the kitchen smelled warm and rich of homemade fruity cake. There was tripe and onions for supper, but Andalusa demanded cake and tea with Nestlé's milk in it. Andalusa had her fancies, and being the only girl, and years younger than her brothers, she was certainly spoiled. But, as Hester said: "If the child won't drink cow's milk, what can you do?"

Having eaten her fill, Andalusa yawned, rubbed her eyes and announced: "I'm going to bed now."

She dipped a spoon into the milk tin and brought it out with the bowl brimful and the milk spilling all up the handle. Hester snatched the tin from her. Andalusa smiled cheekily, put the spoon in her mouth, turned it round, and sucked the handle.

"You limb, you!" exclaimed Hester.

Andalusa slipped off to bed.

Her tiny bedroom was at the back of the farm and overlooked the orchard. The moon was up, and from her window Andalusa could see its rays glimmering on the dew-wet bars of Boxer's cage. Behind the bars were the moonlit boards streaked with thin, slanting shadows, then a glitter of heaped straw, and behind that a motionless, rocklike shape with a spot of light on the end of its nose.

"He's not moved—not one inch," said Andalusa.

When she got into bed she was "pulling that face," as Tom Pagett would have said.

"Flouting me dad, doesn't know when he's well off," she muttered indignantly.

A turbulent lock of hair fell across her mouth. She brushed it away with a sticky little hand. The hand tasted sweet. Andalusa sucked it blissfully. It occurred to her that by a little maneuvering she might manage one night—perhaps tomorrow night—to secrete a whole tin of Nestlé's milk about her person before coming to bed.

"Then I *should* have sweet dreams," she chuckled.

Well, of course, a spanking might follow, but it would be worth it. She was almost asleep when a thought struck her. Bears liked sweet things; probably they liked them as much as she did. If she would sin for Nestlé's milk, surely a bear—even if he had made up his mind to pine away and die—wouldn't be able to resist it?

Wide awake now, she swung her legs out of bed. She was going downstairs to tell her dad to try Boxer with a tin of Nestlé's. Then another, and most exultant idea occurred to her. She wouldn't tell her dad, she would feed Boxer herself, and in the morning prove to them all that she knew a thing or two. Her dad had said that if once they could coax

Boxer to eat anything, he'd get his appetite back and be all right.

"I'll get his appetite back for him," thought Andalusa, "see if I don't."

A great adventure this! Now she must keep herself awake till all the family were abed. She sat with her hands clasped round her knees, and waited. But nobody came upstairs, and surely hours must have gone by! When she found herself nodding and instinctively snuggling down under the bed-clothes, she fetched a chair and put it on her pillow with the legs prodding into her back. That kept her awake for a little while; then she nodded forward. Determinedly she got another chair and placed it on the bed with the legs against her chest.

"Now you can neither lie back nor forth," she told herself.

Hours passed again—or so it seemed to Andalusa. She swayed and drooped into her narrow prison; out of a swoon of sleep the chair legs prodded her, first in her back, then in her chest. And still the family did not come up to their beds.

"Coo!" she muttered drowsily. "This is nearly as bad as that time at Blackpool when the seating c'lapsed, and the fat man fell on top of me."

She slept and dreamed that Boxer was holding a tin of milk over his nose and growling: "More! More!" A chair leg poked her awake and she realized that it was not Boxer, but her father snoring.

"That's all right then," said Andalusa, and got up and felt her way, tiptoeing, down into the kitchen.

The moon was bright outside the uncurtained window, and the whole room was vaguely radiant. Andalusa looked in the store cupboard and counted seven tins of milk, including the one Hester had opened for her tea. She took a basket, climbed on a chair, and reached down the tins. What else? A tin-opener from the table drawer. Could she open tins? Trust Andalusa! A small girl who could already do the splits and the flip-flaps, and ride standing on a pony, was not to be defeated by such a trifle as a tin-opener!

Then her eyes fell upon the brave array of Hester's big cakes, set in the windowsill, covered with a white cloth. One by one those cakes went into the basket, till it was full to the handle. And, so laden, she cautiously opened the back door and stepped out into the moonlight.

"Coo!" said Andalusa. "Isn't this a treat!"

Every grass blade on the rough turf at the end of the yard wore a fiery jewel; the blossom in the orchard was purest snow, and under the trees was such a tangle of dark shadows and gleaming lights that you might fancy yourself performing on some spangled trampolin under the Big Top.

Lion smell, horse smell, blossom smell, wet-grass smell: a line of light showing far off under the closed doors of the elephant shed. But that meant nothing. Andalusa knew that Ferny kept a lamp burning all night because the Queen of Sheba was afraid of mice. She stood still a moment and listened. The night was full of familiar noises: a flump, as one of the big cats turned over in its sleep, the snort of a horse away in the grazing fields, then a gentle wuffling, and the soft stampede of unshod hoofs. Andalusa came with her basket to Boxer's cage.

Boxer was not asleep. He was still sitting against the back wall staring into vacancy. The thick straw glittered, and the moon whitened his eyeballs.

"You'll be dead by morning, if you go on as you're going," said Andalusa severely.

She put down her basket, tore a hunk of cake, tipped sweet milk from the opened tin over it, and held it between the bars.

"Come on," she said, "this is real nice."

She might have been talking to a stone.

"Haven't you got any guts—or what?" asked Andalusa. "It's good, I tell you."

To prove how good it was, she pulled back her hand and took a bite herself; then another bite. But that wouldn't do! She hadn't come out to gorge herself, but to make Boxer eat. Fearful where her greed might lead her, she took aim, flung the sticky cake through the bars, and hit Boxer on the nose.

"That startled you, didn't it?" she said, rather anxiously.

It had startled him; the cake fell at his feet, but the sweetness remained on his nose. He turned his heavy head once or twice from side to side, as if he had just waked up and didn't know where he was. Then, slowly, his tongue came out and licked his nose.

Andalusa gripped the bars with both her hands, and almost held her breath. Boxer had his head down now, he was sniffing, half-heartedly, among the straw.

"There, there—there at your feet!" breathed Andalusa.

Languidly, and after the manner of a reluctant invalid, Boxer put out his tongue again, and licked the cake. Yes, Andalusa was right. He might think he was pining to death, but he couldn't resist the taste of Nestlé's milk, any more than she could. She wanted to shout and skip, but she heroically restrained herself. Not for nothing had she watched wild animals being trained.

"The cake, now the cake—eat it! No need to starve because you said you would. I say things, often I do, and take 'em back!" she whispered urgently.

Would he, or wouldn't he? He didn't seem to know his own mind. Gripping the bars with whitened fingers, Andalusa breathed a prayer. Boxer sniffed the cake, took it in his mouth, dropped it, picked it up again—and swallowed it.

Andalusa heaved an enormous sigh, and immediately became businesslike. "There's plenty more where that came from!" she said, smearing another piece of cake with milk. "Here y'are! But this time you can use your legs—do 'em good!"

Boxer raised his nose to sniff, and his muzzle gleamed.

"You're driveling!" exclaimed Andalusa triumphantly. "Your mouth's watering!"

Boxer's mouth actually was watering, and what was more he was up on his legs, and shambling stiffly across to the bars.

"I could kiss you!" cried Andalusa, as, after a few hesitant rollings of his head, he took the cake from her hand.

It was easy after that, except that the milk tin was soon empty. Andalusa pushed the empty tin through the bars for Boxer to lick out, while she struggled to open another. She cut her fingers on the jagged tin, and blamed the bear for it.

"Here I am cutting myself to pieces for you," she said. "And you are grateful? I don't think!"

Boxer put the tip of his muzzle meekly through the bars, and Andalusa playfully smacked his nose. Then she offered him a whole big cake, dripping with sweet milk. Of course he couldn't pull it through the bars, and it fell onto the wet grass. Andalusa picked it up, broke off a fragment, and pushed it into the cage.

But she was beginning to feel cold, and also impatient. "Shall be here all night at this rate," she said, as she dribbled more cake through the bars. "If the door was open, I'd feed you good and quick."

Well, and why shouldn't the door be open? The bolt was high above her reach, but that difficulty was soon overcome. A pedestal that Josef had been painting stood under an apple tree. Andalusa dragged it over, climbed onto it, and swung the door back.

Then, basket and all, she stepped into the cage.

"Do you know who this is?" she asked Boxer. "This is Andalusa Pagetta, the all-over-the-world famous bear-trainer. Up on your hind legs for Andalusa Pagetta, you great booby! Up, I say! Or you get no more cake from me."

Ho, ho! He *was* up on his hind legs, his huge body towered over her, and his long sharp claws shone silver. Andalusa wished she had an audience; then she was glad she hadn't, for though she held the cake high above her head she couldn't reach anywhere near Boxer's muzzle. He dropped on all fours, and Andalusa, to escape being bowled over by the descending avalanche, backed hurriedly against the bars. With the jerk she gave, the cage door vibrated, swung slowly, swung faster—and clanged shut.

"See what you've done now!" exclaimed Andalusa reproachfully.

Boxer had his head in the basket. He had just discovered how very hungry he was. He took a tin of milk in his paws, sat on his haunches, crushed the tin open with his teeth, and tilting his head back, tipped the milk down his throat. Andalusa watched him with her lips parted. She didn't feel frightened, exactly—it had been drilled into her from babyhood that a Pagett never did feel frightened—but she felt a bit awed. The great, thick-coated beast was so *very* big, and it looked now as if he was out to eat the world.

"Seeing that you've got your appetite back," she announced, "I think I'll be going."

Boxer took no notice whatever. The tin was over his nose, and his tongue was busy at the bottom of it. Standing on tiptoe, Andalusa put her hand to the door catch, but she kept her face to the bear as she knew a good animal-trainer should.

"Good night," she said.

It was only then that she realized that the catch was a tricky one, designed to frustrate any over-curious or over-impulsive occupant of the cage. Do what she would the door would not open. She pulled, she pushed, she rattled, she jerked; forgetting the habits of all good animal-trainers she turned her back on Boxer and fiddled till her fingers were sore. But the catch would not budge, and in the end she gave up trying.

"Well," she said resignedly, pushing the hair back from her face, "seems you and me's got to make a night of it."

Boxer crunched the last tin of milk between his teeth.

"There's all these bits and pieces you haven't eaten yet," said Andalusa, pointing to Boxer's discarded breakfast and supper. "May's well make a clean sweep. But if you hadn't been so greedy, I could do with a piece of cake myself."

At six in the morning, young Jacky, who had risen early to clean out the monkey cage—because he purposed to take the day off with a girl he was sweet on—burst into his parents' room shouting hysterically.

"Our Lu's in the bear's cage!"

"You're crackers!" said Tom Pagett, waked suddenly from soundest sleep and frowning incredulously. But even as he said "You're crackers," he was out of bed and pulling on his trousers.

"She is, I tell you!" cried Jacky. "She's asleep and he's asleep."

Tom Pagett was through the door by this time, and Hester was out of bed and thrusting on her dressing-gown. In less than no time everyone on the farm was assembled outside the bear's cage.

They spoke in whispers as they peered through the bars.

On his bed of straw Boxer lay full length in sleep, with his ponderous forelegs stretched, paws slightly curled, and long murderous-looking claws carelessly extended. And between those claws and the bear's muzzle lay Andalusa, with her head on his broad chest, one arm flung across his neck, and the straw pulled up round her pyjama-clad body. There was not a morsel of food left in the cage, but on the floor there were the crushed remains of seven tins of condensed milk and a broken basket.

"Oh, my God!" whispered Hester Pagett. "When he wakes, he'll kill her!"

"I'll try and snatch her up quick," murmured Tom, "before he realizes. You all stand by with the poles."

They ran for poles. They stood with the pole ends through the bars, ready to thrust back Boxer should he wake to kill.

There might be uproar enough in a few moments, but now they neither moved nor spoke. Tom reached the cage door, opened it with scarcely a sound, and swung himself inside.

It wasn't much of a noise he made as he took a step forward, only the faintest vibration of his feet on the floorboards. But it woke Boxer. He eyed Tom Pagett, and growled.

"Easy then, easy, old fellow!" said Tom.

Boxer growled again.

"He's vicious!" whispered Hester.

But Boxer wasn't really vicious; he was only feeling protective of his new companion. Perhaps it might have come to the same thing as far as Tom Pagett was concerned, but, as Boxer growled again and again, and watched Tom with unwinking eyes, Andalusa woke up.

For a moment, not finding herself in bed, she blinked in amazement. Then she took in the situation: her father's stealthy inching forward, the tense faces outside the cage, the pole ends at the ready, poked through the bars. Yes, she took it all in, and the long generations of her circus ancestry seemed epitomized in the magnificent gesture with which she rose to her feet.

"You're ignorant," she announced superbly. "The whole boiling of you's ignorant. *You* don't know how to manage bears! Eat? 'Course he'll eat! Fetch me some bread, and I'll show you!"

"Come out, Lu, come out for God's sake!" pleaded Hester.

Andalusa gave her mother a queenly smile. Then she stopped and patted Boxer's head.

"I'll bring your breakfast d'reckly," she told him. "*You* aren't going to be sent packing, not today, nor yet tomorrow."

Tom Pagett watched every movement, poised to leap forward at whatever risk to his life, should Boxer turn nasty. But Boxer was feeling full and contented. He had wakened into a realization that life was pleasant, and that he was not friendless after all. He seemed to understand now that his new playmate was not being wrenched from him, but was merely removing herself temporarily and of her own free will. He lifted his massive head and licked her fingers. Then he dropped his head to the straw again and stretched luxuriously.

Andalusa walked proudly to the cage door, and Josef lifted her down. Tom Pagett stepped out after her, and clanged the door shut. Now that the crisis was over, a great burst of laughter seemed to be welling up inside him. Laughter and, yes, pride.

"Our Lu, she doesn't know what fear means," he thought. "And she's got personality. She'll be a stunner on Pagett's come by and by!"

He turned away so that Andalusa should not see how he gloried in her, for she was minx enough already.

But Hester pounced on her small daughter, doubled Andalusa's head under her arm, and began to smack her. The smacking was by no means a light one, Hester had a strong hand and arm, and she was relieving her feelings. However, Andalusa's sense of showmanship did not desert her. The chastisement was taking place in full view of her friend the bear—indeed, as he got up and padded uneasily to the front of the cage, he might be said to have a front seat for the performance. Andalusa peeped at him from under Hester's arm, and her sharp little face, though it shook to the rhythm of the smacking, wore a look both impudent and triumphant.

"Told you I was tough, didn't I?" she shrilled. "Now you see I wasn't speaking a lie . . . I can take it!"

The Trained Kangaroo

BOB BARTON

[as told to G. Ernest Thomas]

When Colonel Miller's show disbanded during the winter of 1897, I had expected to go north again for theater work. But one evening the boss stopped me as I came from the mess tent. "Come along over to my wagon, Bob," he said. "I have something to offer you."

I followed him around the corner of the big tent and over to where his wagon was lined up with the others. We climbed the stairs at the rear and entered the tiny compartment which was both his sleeping room and office.

"People are looking for something new these days," the Colonel began. "We can't go on the road next season with exactly the same show that we had this fall. I am thinking of keeping three or four of you somewhere in South Carolina to work with the animals. Would you care for the job?"

"Would I!" I shouted. "I'll train any kind of animal you can get hold of."

Colonel Miller smiled. "Perhaps you won't be so sure when I tell you that I am having a kangaroo shipped over here from England."

I quickly lost my enthusiasm. "But not a kangaroo!" I exclaimed. "That's impossible."

I told him some of Colonel Hartshorn's stories about his experiences in Australia. He said the kangaroos were the wildest animals he had ever seen. It was difficult for him even to get within gunshot of them. He said he tried many times to capture one, but found them faster than our North American deer.

"Not only that," I continued, "but he said they are mean animals. He saw one hop away from a fight with a huge snake. The snake was crushed to a pulp by the kangaroo's powerful back legs. No," I concluded with a definite shake of my head, "you can't expect us to train a kangaroo."

Colonel Miller waited until I was finished. I was a little angry when I saw that he was smiling.

"Maybe you don't want the job," he said. "Just forget it. I'll get somebody else."

"Wait," I cried, "I didn't mean that I wasn't willing to try. What do you expect me to train the kangaroo to do?"

"I don't know," said the Colonel frankly. "I haven't the least idea just what tricks are possible. A traveling show in England has used a pair for two years now. Perhaps they have done nothing more than exhibit them in a cage. Maybe that is all we shall be able to do with ours, but I have a feeling they can be trained for an act. You go down to Charleston with the others and I'll have the kangaroo shipped there as soon as he arrives in New York. You can work with him and find out what he will be able to do."

I was as impatient as any kid performer while waiting for the kangaroo to arrive. I talked with many of my friends about what stunts I might teach him. No one had any idea.

They all laughed aloud at the very thought of training a kangaroo to take a place in the tent.

Colonel Miller's letter saying that the new performer had been shipped from New York came on the day before he was due to arrive. I could hardly wait until time to go down to the train.

The baggage men lifted the cage out of the car. I ran forward, anxious to get a first glimpse of my new trouper. Even then I could see that he was frightened. The train ride, the bouncing about during the transfer from the baggage car to the truck, and all the strange eyes peering at him had made the kangaroo wild with fear.

I hustled the cage into one of our show wagons and got away from the crowd as soon as possible. It was clear to me that lots of training would be necessary before the kangaroo would be ready for the show. There was hard work ahead, and I was anxious to start it as soon as possible.

The letter from the Colonel had said that bread and milk were good food for a kangaroo, so that evening I prepared his supper with my own hands. I carried it to the cage and set it inside. At first he shrank into the corner and would not come near the dish. When I kept talking in a soft and soothing voice, he began to edge nearer and nearer. He ate his supper while I stood outside the cage only two feet away.

For the next three days I did most of my training when it was time for the kangaroo to eat. It took only a single day to teach him to come quickly for his meal when I put it into the cage. On the second afternoon I was able to reach out my hand and touch him. Time after time he scampered away as soon as he felt my hand on him. At last, however, he stayed to eat his supper while I patted him and talked softly to him.

Those of us who were in the camp had many arguments about the name for the kangaroo. Somebody suggested "Aussie" because he came from Australia. I thought such a name was too hard for children to say and understand.

In the end he was named by a small boy from Charleston

who happened to be on the lot during the kangaroo's first adventure out of his cage. We had erected a corral in which to do the training. We carried the cage into this while the kangaroo was still inside. Then we opened the door.

Only those who have watched a rabbit hop can appreciate how strange the gait of a kangaroo is. We all laughed whenever he took a jump. The small boy who was peering through the fence was carried away with enthusiasm. "Say! Isn't he a bouncer?" he exclaimed.

The word kept coming back. "Bouncer! Bouncer!" I repeated to myself.

"There is a name for him!" I declared. "We'll call him Bouncer."

From then on the kangaroo was Bouncer to all the show people as well as to the boys and girls who came to see him.

This gave me an idea of what the kangaroo would be able to do for an act. He could leap so easily and so high that I felt we might make a tiny platform reaching fifteen or eighteen feet into the air, and teach him to hop up on it. I could even seem to hear the shouts of the crowd when the act was finished and the band struck up a tune.

It was only after many failures that I began to understand Colonel Miller's point of view. Perhaps a kangaroo was intended to be left in the wilds and not to work in an act. I had never used a whip in training animals, but I was sorely tempted to lay one heavily upon the kangaroo's back. It was discouraging to prepare all the equipment for an act only to have Bouncer forget my instructions and chase after a dog or stop to wrestle with Teddy, our trained bear.

Then for several days everything seemed to go well. The platform upon which Bouncer was to jump had been raised from five feet to eight feet, and I felt certain that we could put it up to ten feet before the end of the month. It seemed that the hardest part of the training was over.

But another disappointment was in store for us. One morning Bouncer was mounted upon a small barrel waiting my signal for the great hop to the top of the platform. All my previous commands had been followed and I had every reason to believe we would finish the act successfully. Suddenly Bouncer raised his nose into the air as if smelling the wind. I gave a command to attract his attention, but it went unheard. Without warning the kangaroo hopped off the barrel, took one jump toward the fence, and went over the top with a great leap.

"Help! Help!" I screamed as I ran throught the gate. "Bouncer has—"

I stopped, spellbound. Just before me was Bouncer, wrestling with the trained bear. Evidently he had sensed that Teddy was near and wanted to play. He made no move to run away when I came near, nor did he seem to object when I dragged him back to the corral.

"That kangaroo seems to care for nothing except wrestling," said Billy when I told him about it. "You had better forget the kangaroo act and work on something which will be of use on the road. Bouncer is an interesting animal all right, but he'll never make a performer."

I agreed with Billy at the time and decided to give up the daily training periods. But that night as we sat around the fire, I had an idea. At first it seemed so silly that I didn't mention it to the others.

Later in the evening I found courage enough to speak up about it. "What would you say," I asked, "to our working out a boxing act for the kangaroo? He is playful and seems to like to punch anyone in sight. Perhaps we could teach him to do some real boxing. It surely would be good for a few laughs."

My friends all thought the plan was foolish, while admitting that it would be a hit if the kangaroo would box or wrestle with his trainer.

"But it wouldn't be worth the trouble," concluded Billy. "You never could depend upon Bouncer to do his part."

Billy's opinion sounded reasonable, yet I thought about the

idea a great deal in the next few days. Then another sugges-
tion seemed worth trying. I didn't tell anyone about it, but I
asked Harry Burton to make a pair of purple tights to fit
Bouncer. Then I went downtown to find some boxing gloves
large enough to go on the kangaroo's front paws.

Bouncer objected strongly to wearing the tights and gloves.
He whaled me with both his front paws and tore his first pair
of silk tights to shreds. I was patient, however, and it was not
long until Bouncer was dressed and ready for a workout. All
of us laughed at him. He looked with sad eyes at one glove
and then the other. He worked desperately trying to yank
them off.

After putting on a pair of gloves myself, I walked over
toward the kangaroo. I touched him lightly with my glove
and then lifted his paw the second time against my chest. A
third time I punched him easily and this time it was not necessary for me to lift his paw. He had already struck me.

It was surprising how quickly Bouncer learned to box. He
had seemed so dumb when we tried to teach him the trapeze
act that no one felt he would learn to handle the gloves. The
truth of the matter was that Bouncer was not taught to box.
He took to it naturally. He boxed as he played. The act was a
good one because it was a natural.

The kangaroo was often very funny without intending to
be. One day we were milling about in the corral. He was
striking me often, though usually not very hard. His greatest
fault lay in his attempts to come close enough to hug me. I
had a feeling that such a habit might spoil the act, so whenever he threw his front legs around my neck, I hit him rather
hard with my boxing gloves. This day he was very friendly
and got a grip around my neck which it was almost impossible
to break. Partly in self-defense and partly because I wanted
to teach him to keep away, I struck Bouncer very hard. The
kangaroo slid away from me and sat down heavily on the
ground. He looked up as if uncertain what to do next. He
blinked his eyes and looked first at me and then at his gloves.

I was afraid that my unintended blow had ruined our act, for when I went over to help him up, Bouncer scampered away on all fours. He had evidently had enough. It took all the persuasion of nearly a full box of sugar before he would again exchange blows. The sugar had a magic way with him, though, and Bouncer would do almost anything to get it. He forgot his hurts and was soon busy again with his boxing.

The first time the kangaroo act was used in the tent it caused a great sensation. I wore bright-yellow tights and arranged to have the act announced as if it were a championship fight. The crowd howled with laughter when we entered the ring. Bouncer carried on like an old trouper. He did every part of the act as we had planned it. When the time came for him to strike the blow which was to send me to the sawdust, he delivered it with considerable strength. He jumped up and down with glee as I lay on the ground.

Bouncer was not as dependable as some of the other animals in the show. There was always the possibility that he would do something unexpected. He had no formal stunts. The boxing act, however, allowed for his strange ways.

Our kangaroo didn't play his part only in the tent. He was a boxer all the time. He was apt to strike anyone who interfered with what he wanted to do. On one occasion, however, he tried to use his skill to help a friend.

Bouncer had become very fond of Billy. I was walking around the grounds one evening holding the kangaroo by a chain when suddenly we came upon a strange sight. It was Billy's birthday and some of the boys were tossing him in the air in a blanket.

Billy was shouting: "Hey, that's enough! Let me down!" Bouncer thought he was calling for help. He broke away from me and hopped over to the crowd. Then he began punching right and left. His blows were not hard and the boys took it in good fun. I couldn't help admiring the loyalty of the kangaroo to the one he recognized as his friend.

It was always great fun to give Bouncer a bath. Show people often went down to some brook or stopped beside a lake to wash. Most animals dislike the water, and Bouncer was no exception. For some time it was impossible to get him close to it. The best we could do was to lead him down to the edge of the stream and there sponge him off. Gradually, however, Bouncer began of his own choice to wade into the water a short distance. It was not long before he enjoyed every chance to splash in a stream. We always heard his strange and pitiful cry if we went bathing without him.

The kangaroo was a peculiar beast. Many of the show people were certain, at first, that they could never become very fond of him. But Bouncer was loyal to all his friends, and came to be one of the best-loved animals in the show.

"Mis"

NOEL STREATFEILD

It was in Sheffield in the third week in May that Mis got sick. The children heard of it when, with Fritzi and Hans, they went to fetch Fifi for school. Usually Fifi was dressed and ready, waiting to shake hands and say good morning in her polite way. Today there was not a sign of her, in spite of their knocking. Then suddenly she came running from the direction of the stables. Her face was white and her eyes red with crying.

"Something wrong was?" said Fritzi nervously. She gripped Peter's arm.

Usually Peter hated to have his arm held, but this time he was so worried he did not notice it.

Long moments passed before they could find out what had happened. The moment Fifi began to tell them she cried, and all they could hear was "Mis."

At last Fritzi asked a direct question. "Mis was gone dead?"

Fifi raised her head.

"No, but she was very sick."

Santa was sorry about Mis, but she did not think it would help if they were all late for school. She took Fifi's arm. "I imagine she'll be all right. Come on. Perhaps when we get back she'll be better."

They were a very drooping procession going to school. Even Sasha and Olga, who joined them, had not the heart to do more than walk quietly. The illness of a dog of Mis's ability took the spirit out of them all.

"How did it start?" asked Olga. "Santa and me and Peter were in front last night. Mr. Cob passed us in. She wasn't ill then."

"It must have started in the night. It was early in the morning that *Maman* sat up. She woke Papa. 'Quick!' she said. 'Mis is ill. I feel it here.'" Fifi clasped the place where her heart was, to show what her mother had done.

"How did she know?" Peter asked. "Did she hear her whining?"

Olga, Sasha, Fritzi, Hans, and Fifi looked at him. Their faces showed they thought he had said something very silly.

"With us," Olga explained severely, "our animals are the same as children. If a baby is put to bed its mother may go to sleep and not worry. But suddenly in the night she'll wake up, and some little thing that was different will come to her. 'My baby is ill,' she'll say. Then she'll run. So it is with us."

"Well, but Mis wasn't different last night," Peter objected. "We saw her. She was just the same as usual."

"To you, yes," Fifi agreed. "But not to *Maman*. And she was right." She lowered her voice dramatically. "Papa ran to the stables. He went to Mis's kennel. She lay still. At first he thought she was sleeping. Then he laid his hand on her. She was stiff and cold. She was unconscious."

"Goodness!" Santa was appalled at the thought of energetic, lively Mis lying unconscious. "What did your father do?"

"*Maman* had followed him. They picked Mis up. They wrapped her in blankets. They poured water on her head.

Presently she opened her eyes. Then *Maman* fed her with the white of an egg beaten with brandy. They feel her to see if she has any pain. They think that perhaps she has been poisoned."

"Poisoned!" all the children exclaimed.

Fifi made a gesture to show that anything was possible. "Where there is so great an *artiste* there is always jealousy."

"Well, had she been?" asked Peter.

"No. That very day there had been new kennels. Better in front. It is impossible for anyone to pass anything through. Besides, Mis has no trouble inside. She has no fever. It is just that she's unhappy. She cries and cries. My papa fetches a vet. A very good vet. He can find nothing. But today she's no better. Her lovely coat doesn't shine. She won't eat. She won't drink."

Sasha pulled her sleeve.

"Will she be in the show today?"

Fifi shrugged her shoulders and raised her hands.

"Who knows? She cannot go on the parade this morning. She won't leave her kennel."

"Perhaps the air of Sheffield disagrees with her," Santa suggested.

Fifi shook her head.

"It's worse than that. Sometimes it may be the place doesn't suit. But then a little powder and all is well. *Maman* says she remembers now that since Sunday when we arrived she has been quiet."

"Nobody has brought a dog near her, have they?" Olga asked. "Could she have caught anything? You know, she might have."

"Perfectly," Fifi agreed. "But if that was so she would have fever. Nor has she a chill. On Sunday, when the stables are built, there was a dip in the ground where the dogs are put to play when the menagerie is shown. So Papa went to Monsieur Schmidt and asked if for this one week he will change places. So he puts his sea lions at the end next to the elephants."

Fritzi and Hans had heard of this change. Mr. and Mrs.
Schmidt had agreed to it, but at home they had sniffed and
said the fuss the Moulins made about their dogs was ridiculous. There had been no rain for days to make the dip damp.
However, this was no moment to say anything about being
fussy. Fritzi and Hans merely looked at each other and said
nothing.

After school they all hurried home. They followed Fifi to
the stables. Both Mr. Moulin and Lucille were sitting by
Mis's kennel. The other dogs were playing about in an enclosure in the sun outside, but Mis lay in her basket with lack-
luster eyes. The children looked expectantly at Mr. Moulin
and Lucille. Lucille got up and came to them. Even in a moment of crisis like this she could not forget her manners.

"Good morning, Fritzi and Hans. Good morning, Peter
and Santa."

They all spoke at once.

"Good morning. How is Mis?"

Lucille shrugged her shoulders and raised her hands. Her
eyes filled with tears.

"Sick."

"What's the matter with her?" asked Santa.

Lucille sighed. "Who can say? The vet can find nothing."

"Perhaps it's a mood," Olga suggested.

"That may be," Lucille agreed. "I have said I believe she
is suffering here." She held her heart.

"But why should she?" Peter argued. "Nothing's happened."

Lucille sighed again.

"Who can say? With a great *artiste* it may be a little thing.
They are such children. Once we have a dog; she was a dog
from Holland. A very clever dog, but to us she was quiet.
'She has no temperament, that one,' I said. My husband said:
'She has temperament, but she is a Hollander. Hollanders do
not show how they feel.' He was right. One day that dog is
sick. She cannot eat. The next day it is the same. She takes

nothing, but nothing at all. That night I wake up. I wake my husband. I say: 'I know how it is that Gretchen will not eat. Come, I will show you.' We get up and go to the stables. The watchman brings us a light. Gretchen is asleep in her basket in her kennels. I have with me some bread in hot milk. I call 'Vooruit. Gretchen, vooruit!' Gretchen jumps up. She comes to me. She eats. You see how it was. We had that week finished teaching her to speak French. We taught her so well that we spoke it to her altogether. In the ring she would not mind, but now we are speaking it for her food. That made her homesick. She will not eat. After that we speak Hollander and she is not sick again."

Peter looked puzzled.

"But you haven't talked anything but French to Mis, have you?"

"But no. But it may be some little thing has hurt her feelings. She is so sensitive, that one."

Fifi took her mother's hand. "Will she work today, Maman?"

Lucille stooped and kissed Fifi's anxious face.

"Yes. She will work. She is the artiste born. It will be in the ring as if there was nothing wrong. Now you must smile, my little one. Come, I have a nice déjeuner waiting for you."

Mis was able to work at both shows. She gave her usual witty performance. Whatever her trouble, she never let the audience know anything was wrong.

Early the next morning, when Peter went for his riding lesson, he went to the kennels to inquire for her. Violette, Simone, and Marie were playing about in their enclosure outside. Mr. Moulin was hanging their blankets up to air. There was no sign of Mis. Peter felt a sinking inside as if he were going down in an elevator. No Mis. Had she died in the night? Mr. Moulin read his thoughts.

"It's all right, Peter. We took her to sleep in the caravan."

"Is she better this morning?"

Mr. Moulin fastened leads onto Violette, Simone, and Marie. His face was sad.

"No."

Nothing could take away Peter's pleasure in his riding lesson, but inside he had that dull ache you get when something is wrong, even if you are not actually thinking about it.

He was getting on well with his riding. He needed no help to mount Mustard now. Ben had taken away his stirrups. He did not believe you could be considered a rider unless you could trot without them.

"Movin' by slow ways, that's my method," he said. "No stirrups now, not till August. Before then I'll put you up on a lot of diff'rent 'osses. You've got to ride 'em when they're lively, and difficult to handle. When I can put you on any 'oss in the stables and you can make 'im know from the beginnin' you're not one he can take liberties with, then we'll be gettin' somewhere."

"What'll I do in August?" Peter asked.

Ben chewed his straw thoughtfully.

"Maybe I'll see how you shape at high school."

Peter was so surprised he felt as if somebody had hit him in the wind. *Haute école,* of which Alexsis had said: "This is the most best work in riding."

"Do you mean what the Kenets and Paula do?"

Ben nodded.

"By the time I was second head of the stables I was teachin' it. It's pretty work for the 'osses, and fine control for the riders."

"But it's proper circus riding. Could I?"

Ben moved his straw across to the other side of his mouth.

"From all I hear, it wasn't always used in a circus. There was a gentleman come round once. Artist he was. Always paintin' the 'osses. Tented with us one or two summers. He told me that in the time of Oliver Cromwell—you know him in the history books—his special bodyguard was all trained in it. The artist told me it was a right good idea. He said the passes left and right were just the thing for fightin' with a sword."

Peter tried to picture himself fighting with a sword on horseback. He saw a mental figure of himself dressed as a Roundhead, his sword thrusting left and right. And as he moved, he saw the horse moving with him.

"It would be a good thing to do. It would be much better than an ordinary horse that only goes backwards and for-wards."

"That's right." Ben sucked his straw meditatively. "Mind you, it's true. I heard tell there was a statue to King Charles that had a 'oss doin' high-school work. So last time I was at the winter stables I took a day off and went up to see. I had the name of the place written on a bit of paper."

"Did you find it all right?"

Ben nodded.

"Very nice it was, too. Nicely trained the 'oss seemed. Must 'ave come hard on him, posin' that long. It's 'ard enough to get a 'oss to hold his position while his photo's taken. Shouldn't care for the job of keepin' 'im quiet while they made a statue of 'im."

"Can I start at the beginning of August? When my holidays begin?"

"Maybe. We'll see how you shape. You keep your legs down better. Sittin' the way I often see you, with your toes turned in, you couldn't use a spur. I'd 'ave my 'osses ripped raw."

"You wouldn't!" Peter said indignantly.

Ben never noticed when people were cross; his voice was as slow and mild as usual.

"Couldn't 'elp it, son. If your toes are turned in, then you force the calves of your legs out. Sittin' that way your 'oss won't feel your leg before the spur the way he should. And when you 'ave to use the spur, it won't be a gentle touch as is proper, you'll 'ave to jab. Sittin' that way, you can't do anythin' else."

Peter longed to argue. He was certain Ben was wrong. If only he had some spurs on, he would show him. But it was a waste of time arguing with Ben. He never seemed to notice you were arguing. He never supposed anyone would want to argue with him about horses or riding.

After the lesson Peter went with Mustard to his stall. He gave him a pat and some carrots, and walked down the stables. He liked it there. He knew most of the stable lads by name now. At this hour of the morning they were all about. Doing the stables. Cleaning the harness. Grooming the horses. The *Bereiters* leading the different horses into the ring for exercise. There was a nice cheerful noise of hissing during the grooming. The horses stamped. There was a good smell of stables. Usually most of the men had a word to say, but this morning they were all gossiping among themselves. Peter stopped by the stable lad he knew best.

"Has something happened, Nobby?"

Nobby pretended to be intent on Magician's hind legs, which he was brushing. He spoke quietly.

"There's trouble with one of the elephants."

"Which elephant?"

"Ranée. The little one on the end of the line."

"What's the matter with her?"

"Turned nasty-tempered. Got at one of the men this morning and threw him down. If Mr. Cob hears of it he won't let her work. He'd never 'ave one you couldn't trust in the ring."

"But all the elephants are good-tempered. I always feed them."

"Well, you better not get too near Ranée today, or you may get something you don't expect."

"Funny her getting suddenly angry."

Nobby gave Magician a slap.

"Get over, can't you?" He gave a glance in the direction of the elephants. "It all comes of keepin' wild beasts. You give me 'orses. You knows where you are with them."

Peter walked toward the elephants. Kundra was talking to the head keeper. From a cautious distance he had a look at Ranée. As far as he could see she was exactly as usual. She swayed from side to side. Her trunk was held out hopefully on the chance that some passer-by might have a fragment to give away.

"Well," Kundra was saying, "give her that with her food. Maybe the weather has upset her. These spring days are apt to get them a bit down."

"Right," the keeper agreed. He and Kundra went out of the tent. They were talking so busily they never noticed Peter.

From his safe position Peter went on looking at Ranée. He felt sorry for her. Perhaps she was feeling as Ben said Mustard felt in the early autumn. Ben said Mustard missed the smell of falling leaves and would go off his food. Was Ranée missing the smell of new plants coming up? Peter had very vague ideas about the kind of country elephants were used to. Jungles, he supposed. He did not know what grew in jungles, but whatever it was probably got new leaves in the spring. Perhaps Ranée missed the smell of them. He felt in his pocket. He had a few carrots. There were always carrots in the caravan and he took some to give Mustard.

These were spare ones. It would be nice to give them to Ranée to cheer her up. But he did not at all want to be thrown on the ground. He took a few steps forward. Ranée did not look cross. He took another few steps. He got the carrots out. Perhaps if she saw he was bringing carrots she would know he meant to be nice. Three more steps and he could reach her. He looked around. Nobody was about. If he went back to the caravan now, nobody would know he had meant to give Ranée carrots and had not because he was afraid. He stood irresolute for a second. Should he go home? Then he looked at Ranée. She must have seen the carrots. It would be mean to take them away now. He took the steps forward. He held out his hand.

Ranée took the carrots. She put them in her mouth. She

crunched them up. But although she ate them and seemed to enjoy them, Peter got the impression that tidbits were not what she was asking for. He forgot to be frightened. He put his hand on her trunk. He had often done it to the elephants before. Sometimes one of them would hold him so he had to pull to get free. Ranée did that now. She put her trunk around his arm. After a moment he gave a little pull to get free. She held him tighter. He gave his arm a tug. Ranée not only gripped him more firmly, she pulled him toward her.

"Let go, Ranée!"

Ranée had no intention of doing anything of the kind. She drew Peter forward. His feet touched the wooden platform on which the elephants stood. He was cold with fright. At any moment he expected to be picked up and thrown to the ground. He pulled. He struggled. But it's not much use struggling with an elephant.

"Let go, Ranée!" he gasped. "Let go!"

He looked up. He was staring into her eyes. Elephants' eyes are not the sort most people admire. That small, pig-like shape is not handsome. Standing as close to them as Peter was, he thought they looked awful. Then suddenly he saw something in them which surprised him. He had thought they looked fierce and cruel. Now, seeing them more closely, he saw they were miserable. He was so sorry for her he forgot the way she was treating him.

"Poor Ranée," he said. "Poor old girl."

It looked as if a little sympathy was just what Ranée wanted. As suddenly as she had gripped his arm, she let it go. Peter, instead of moving out of her range, stood where he was. He fondled her trunk. He looked around. What could she be miserable about? The stable was as usual. On the left the ponies munched their breakfast. On the right came pleased, hoarse barks from the sea lions' wagon. Then suddenly he had an idea.

Kundra and the keeper came back. They stood staring at Peter. Kundra came forward gently.

"Don't be frightened, Peter. Move slowly backward away from Ranée. She's in a bad mood this morning."

Peter stayed where he was. He went on fondling Ranée's trunk.

"I know, but I don't believe she has a bad mood. I think she's unhappy."

"Maybe." Kundra still talked in a quiet voice. "But do what I say. Come toward me slowly."

Peter still did not move. He looked around again at the sea lions' wagon. He was shy of saying what he thought because, of course, everybody in the circus knew about animals and he did not.

"Could an elephant be fond of a dog?"

Kundra and the keeper knew at once what he meant. They looked at the sea-lion wagon standing in the position where the poodles always played.

"I wonder," said Kundra. "Something's upset Mis."

The keeper nodded.

"D'you remember that lion we had out with us? The Rajah of Bong? Remember that little fox terrier he had alongside of him? Had to live in his cage?"

"It can happen," Kundra agreed. "There have been some funny friends. My father had one elephant who made friends with a pony."

"Shall I fetch Mr. Moulin?" the keeper suggested.

"Yes." Kundra beckoned to Peter. "Come on, son. You may be right, but she's bashed one of the men's arms this morning and we don't want to take you to hospital too."

Peter gave Ranée a final pat. He moved away from her. She made no effort to hold him. He had a feeling she had been listening to the conversation and was pleased with him.

A smell of bacon blew in through the tent door. It woke Peter up to the time.

"Do you know what the time is?"

Kundra looked at his watch.

"Ten minutes past eight."

"Goodness!" Peter started to run. "I shall be late for breakfast."

"Aren't you going to wait and see if you're right about Mis?"

"I can't," Peter called over his shoulder. "I have to go to school."

Peter scuttled out of his jodhpurs and into his shorts. He raced across to the caravan. Gus and Santa were having breakfast.

"What's happened to you?" said Gus. "Breakfast is eight when there's school, and you know it."

"Sorry." Peter helped himself to bacon and eggs. "I was talking to the elephants."

Santa gave his back a shocked look. Peter was getting into very bad habits, she thought. He need not have told Gus he had been riding, but he could have said feeding the horses. He always gave Mustard carrots, so it would be true.

Never had Peter so hated going to school. To make it worse Fifi stayed away; at least, when they went to fetch her she was not in the caravan. Nobody was there. Fritzi and Hans, who were with Peter and Santa, looked disgusted.

"Such a fuss about that dog to make. Mine father say she not ill was," Fritzi muttered.

"It was true," Hans agreed. "She was spoilt."

"I don't believe it," Santa argued. "You don't faint just because you're spoilt."

"But yes," Hans explained. "When there is temperament it might be."

Peter said nothing. He looked toward the stables. He wished he were there. He could not tell the others what he thought was wrong. Somehow, now that he was out of doors, doing a prosaic thing like walking to school, the idea seemed ridiculous. They would probably laugh.

Fifi came to school late. Peter did not, of course, see her until they were all going home.

"Imagine," she called out to them. "Mis is well. It was an affair of the heart. She has such affection, that little one. And she had given it to Ranée. Nobody knew. Always they have been placed side by side. Now she is back by her friend and all is well."

"What, Ranée the elephant?" asked Hans.

"Yes," Fifi said, prancing up the road. "It was at breakfast. There comes a knock on our door. *Maman* hold her heart. She has a migraine since Mis is ill. She cannot bear any noise."

Olga turned a cartwheel.

"Was it Ranée come to say she was missing Mis?"

Sasha giggled. He did a flip-flap.

"Did Ranée and Mis kiss each other?"

"*Imbécile!*" Fifi retorted. "No, it was the keeper. He comes to say that Kundra and he have a thought."

Peter gasped.

"He came to say what?"

Fifi sighed at his stupidity.

"He came to tell us of the idea that Ranée and Mis might be friends."

Peter could not believe it.

"He said that he and Kundra had thought of it?"

Fifi nodded.

"But yes. Who else?"

As soon as they got to the ground Peter hurried to the stables. The sea lions had been moved. The poodles were back in their old playground by the elephants. A lot of people who had paid to see the menagerie were passing through. It took a minute before Peter could get close to the poodles' enclosure. When he got there he found Kundra talking to Lucille and Mr. Moulin.

"But it was wonderful," said Lucille. "How was it we did not think? You have a very great understanding of animals, monsieur."

Kundra smiled in a pleased way.

"Oh, well, I've been in the business a long time. One senses things, you know." He stopped, catching Peter's eye. He turned red.

The Moulins, after saying a few more polite words, moved off to have their *déjeuner*. Kundra looked at Peter. He grinned.

"I know, son. But it's no good my saying you thought of it. It's no good to you. You aren't going to train elephants."

"What good is it to you?"

"Mr. Cob is thinking of renewing our contract for another three years."

"Oh!" Peter stopped feeling angry. It was not fair, of course, but at least Kundra was not pretending with him.

Kundra felt in his pocket. He brought out a ten-shilling note. He handed it to Peter.

"Spend that. You've done me a good turn."

Kundra went out of the stables. Peter stared at the note. He did not really want it, though, of course, it was grand to have money to spend. He hated having been given it in exchange for what was more or less a lie. He liked Kundra and wished he had not pretended. Then he looked at Mis and Ranée. Mis had her paws on the fence dividing the poodles from the elephants. Her tongue was hanging out. She looked her amusing gay self. Ranée had her head turned toward her. It was obvious the friends were having a good gossip.

Peter put the note in his pocket. What did it matter who had the thought that separating them might be the trouble? All that really mattered was that Mis and Ranée were their old selves again. He walked off whistling.

Mr. Tidy Paws

FRANCES CLARKE SAYERS

The long and snowy winter came to an end at last. March flooded the earth with melting snow and ice, and April's wind whistled the pussy willows into feathery bloom. The silver birch broke with bud.

On May Day Christopher arose early, and going to the brim of the river, and into the wood, found a few blossoms of the first-to-come spring flowers: hepaticas, violets, spring beauties, and one small bleeding heart. These he gathered into a bouquet, and put them at his Gran's place at the break-fast table to tell her that at long last, spring was walking through the fields.

That May Day night, Christopher made a discovery. What strangely awoke him, in the middle of his deep sleep, he never knew. But he found himself suddenly wide awake, sitting bolt upright in his bed, his ears filled with a strange sound.

He was greatly excited, though he couldn't tell why, and without thinking, without knowing what he was about, he jumped from his bed, put on a pair of carpet slippers, and ran out of the house by the back door, his nightshirt flapping about his heels. He ran beyond the orchard, because the strange sound that was filling his ears came from that direction. He ran until he came to a stretch of meadow, at the margin of the wood. There was a light about the place, and the shrill sound that had been ringing in his ears was at its highest pitch here. It was a sound like laughter, and yet thinner, and more shrill, than any laughter Christopher's ears had known before. And Christopher saw, too, a bright circle of deep, green grass, as lush and long as the grass of midsummer. All the ground was as yet brownish, covered with the straggling growth of early spring, save this one circle of green. Christopher was frightened, though there was nothing he could see to frighten him, but everything was strange: the light, the long, lush grass, the sound he was hearing. This patch of ground, this wood, this earth, he well knew; but it was changed now, and he was afraid. He dropped to his stomach behind a rise of ground, and buried his head in his arms. The shrill, little laughter went on ringing in his ears, but since no harm seemed to come to him, he at length lifted his head and peered above the edge of his small hiding. And there he saw Secret. Secret, his own cat. But what a Secret! He stood in the very center of that green circle of grass, and he stood on his hind legs. He held his front paws across his furry belly, and threw back his head, laughing. He shook himself with his own mirth, but there was no sound coming from him. It was not his laughter that Christopher heard.

Then Secret marched about the circle, still on his hind legs, like a great general. One-two, one-two, he marched, to a new sound, the sound of clapping hands, the sound of a thousand little, little hands clapping. Now Secret stopped, and, drawing himself up proudly, saluted with his black paws, touching right paw to right ear first, then left paw to left ear. Then he turned somersaults, and paw-springs, tail after head, head after tail, until he was a ball of fur rolling around the green circle. And then—Christopher could scarce believe his eyes—Secret stood erect once more, and fell to dancing a merry jig, on his two hind feet, jigging and turning, turning and jigging, and Christopher stuffed his hand into his mouth to keep from laughing his own, human laughter.

Next Secret stood upon his front paws, waving his tail and his hind legs uselessly in the air. There were shouts of laughter and little shrieks of joy. But these were short-lived, for suddenly the air was pierced by a loud and pain-filled "Meow" from Secret, and Christopher, watching him, wondered who was tormenting him. His tail was stiff, his hair on end, his ears twitching. Someone was pinching him and pulling his fur. He gave a great leap into the air, and scampered off, out of the circle, into the night-dark woods. And the laughter followed him, and the light was gone from the place, and Christopher found himself lying on the cold ground, in a night which was deeply dark and without a sound. He lay there a long time, shaken with fright and cold. At last his courage caught up with him, and rising from the ground, he ran back through the house, straight to his grandmother's bed.

"Gran," he cried, "wake up, wake up. I've seen Secret, dancing . . ." He could say nothing further, gasping for breath as he was. His Gran awoke to find Christopher sitting on her bed shivering and wide-eyed, hugging his knees. She was as shivery and wide-eyed herself after she had heard all that Christopher had to tell.

"Christopher," she said, "light a candle, there, on the chest of drawers." Christopher did as he was told, and then came back to be wrapped up in his Gran's crazy-quilt. "Lucky for you, my lad," she said, "that you couldn't see them. For that would have been the end of us. For all you tell me—the shrill laughter, the green ring, the clapping hands—all you tell me convinces me that this night you have looked upon the revels of the little people. Fairies, Christopher! That's what they were." She was whispering now. "And Christopher," and she pulled his head down close to her mouth, "it explains all the strangeness of Secret. He's a changeling cat."

"What?" said Christopher, not knowing what his Gran was saying.

"He's a fairy's cat, and no proper human cat at all. They stole a human cat from somewhere, and set Secret down in your path as an exchange. I've heard of it happening often to children, but this time, bless us, if it isn't a cat that's the changeling."

"What will we do, Gran? Shall we be bewitched?"

"Do?" said Gran, and her voice was firm now. "We'll stand our ground, that's what we'll do. But Christopher, we'll say nothing about this. No one must know, for in matters of this kind it is always wise never to let the tongue know what the eyes have seen. Breathe no word of this night's doing to anyone, and if Secret should come back, we must treat him as though we knew nothing of his true character. And Christopher, when the wild strawberries ripen, and you go out to pick them, be careful to leave some of the largest and ripest hanging on the vines. That will make their wee mouths water! If we guard their secrets, and remember them now and then, they will leave us alone, I'm thinking, and curdle no milk that comes from our cow. Ah, this is a night of wonder, now, isn't it? Here, lad, blow out the candle, and crawl under the covers with me, and go to sleep."

But Christopher's head was so filled with all the marvels that there was no sleep in him, and he lay beside his Gran, still shivering, until the daylight began to come in the window. Then he fell asleep.

When he awoke, his Gran was calling him to breakfast. And when he had dressed himself, and went down the stairs to the breakfast table, there was Secret, licking himself, by the fireplace. Christopher looked at his Gran with a sharp eye.

She was humming a little tune under her breath, and acting very much as she did on other mornings.

"Well," she said, "old Mr. Tidy Paws has come home." That was all they said between them. Christopher poured out a bowl full of cream, took it over to the fireplace, and set it down before Secret.

CHRISTOPHER SEEKS HIS FORTUNE

The wild strawberries were thick across the fields that year. They hung, like little red lanterns, close to the ground. Christopher, with his basket, spent day after day gathering them. Home he came at night, his basket high with the honey-sweet fruit, his mouth red at the corners with their juice.

His grandmother cooked strawberries in six different ways, making jams and jellies and preserves, and strawberry short-cakes, and strawberry stew, until the house was filled with their fragrance, and there was no empty pot, bowl, jar, or jug on the pantry shelf.

But if there were plenty of berries, there was one thing of which there was lack, and that was money. Christopher came home one day to find his Gran staring sadly into the old blue teapot, where the coins were kept, and he knew from the stoop of her shoulders that the teapot was empty.

"Christopher," she said, "make the most of this summer in Bean Blossom, for I think before another winter comes we shall have to follow the others and make a new home in Jeremiad. For there's one thing we must have, if we are to live in this world, and that is money. And there are no silver coins to be picked up here."

Christopher said: "Oh Gran, we can't leave now, after living through the hardest winter Bean Blossom has ever seen." But when he talked about it further, he knew his Gran was right. In the old days, she had been able to earn all they needed, which was little enough, by selling her cookies and brown bread to the neighbors. There was no one in the village of Bean Blossom who could bring from the oven such spicy cookies, such featherweight cake, such crumpets and tarts as Betsy Tree. But now there were no neighbors to buy, and Christopher knew that there were certain things, such as a new roof, or a suit of clothes, which only money could bring.

"We'll have a fine, fair summer of it here, lad," his Gran said. "And this is only early June. The winter is far away. Think no more about it, Christopher."

But Christopher thought of nothing else. He couldn't ride old Conrad across the fields, or go in search of sassafras root, or swim in the Briar Berry River, without thinking of what his Gran had said, without knowing that neither he nor his Gran could ever be happy, Bean Blossom left behind. At last he thought of a plan. One morning he said: "I'm going down the road, Gran. For the summer, I mean. I'll find work to do, and they'll pay me with silver, and then I'll come back and we can stay in Bean Blossom."

His Gran said: "You can't go seeking your fortune, Christopher. You're only a boy."

"But I'm strong, Gran, and I can do many useful things. I'll be gone for only a month or two. You'll not be alone for long. Let me go, Gran."

Betsy Tree couldn't decide which would be the greater sorrow: to lose Bean Blossom forever, or to lose Christopher for a month or two. She said: "No, Christopher, you cannot go."

For the first time in his life Christopher paid no heed to his Gran. He straightway made his plans, working to get everything in order, for his leave-taking, so that Betsy Tree would have little to do while he was gone. His Gran saw at last that he would go, whether or no, and she said to him: "Christopher, in this matter you seem to have a wisdom of your own, and I'll not stand in your way." And she set about making shirts for him, out of her best calico.

The day came when Christopher must start. He set out upon the road, feeling very proud, in his stout walking boots, his clothes tied up in his Gran's plaid shawl and hung from a stick over his shoulder. Betsy watched him as he walked down the road between the poplars. Christopher could think of nothing to call to her, as she stood there. "Say good-by to Secret," he shouted. "I couldn't find him." His Gran nodded her head, and waved. He called good-by once more, and then, turning his face down the road, he trudged away, never daring to look back.

It was the very peak of summer now. Phlox were blooming, and every ditch and hollow was filled with that straight-growing flower his Gran called "butter and eggs." Christopher felt stout in his heart, and gay in his head. He sang some, and whistled a bit, and walked silently, silently to the tune of his boots in the dust of the road. There were other sounds that went with him: a bird now and then, and a certain whispering among the grasses beside the road, made, Christopher supposed, by the passing of some frightened rabbit or running gopher.

All that day Christopher walked, and there was no sign of house or habitation. He rested at noon, eating heartily of the luncheon his Gran had packed for him. And his evening meal, too, he ate by the side of the road. As the sun sank, Christopher realized that he would have to spend his first night away from home under the dark sky. He settled himself beneath a pine tree, and wrapped his Gran's plaid shawl about him. He was very tired, now, and he could not keep his mind from turning back to Bean Blossom and his Gran. He remembered how she looked in the candlelight, setting out the blue and yellow bowls on the table. He remembered the clock shelf above the fireplace, and the tick of the clock. He was homesick. And now that the darkness covered him, he put his head on his knees and cried.

A strange thing happened, then. He felt something soft brush against his legs, something soft touch his hand. He raised his head. There was Secret, nothing of him to be seen in the dark but his gleaming eyes, and his little red tongue

when he opened his mouth to cry "Meow." Then Christopher
knew that the whispering sounds he had heard all day in the
grasses had been Secret's four paws, following him when he
went to seek his fortune.

"Oh Secret!" he said, catching the cat in his arms. "It's
you." And he put his face down into the soft fur of Secret's
back. "It's a hard thing to be sick with thinking of your
home," he said. Secret licked his hand with his rough tongue.
Secret knew.

CHRISTOPHER FINDS A PLACE FOR HIMSELF

Day after day Christopher and Secret trudged down the
leafy road. They stopped at every farmhouse, where Christopher asked for work. Everyone welcomed them. "Mom," the
farmers would shout to their wives, "here's a little boy, with
his cat. Give them something to fatten their bones." But
though there was plenty to eat, black cherries, raspberries
swimming in bowls of rich cream, pears and peaches and
yellow bantam corn, yet everywhere it was very much as it
had been at home: plenty of food but lack of money.

Christopher and Secret could have earned their board
and lodging ten times over, for almost any farmer can find
chores for a boy to do, and every farmer's barn is filled with
unwelcome mice. But Christopher knew that what he needed
was silver coin, with which to cover the bottom of the old
blue teapot at home.

So he and Secret set foot and paw upon the road, hoping
to find some work to do. Christopher found that a third person walked with them now, and that was Old Man Fear, for
Christopher thought that the end of the summer might return them to Bean Blossom, fat with the good food of the
generous country people, but without one piece of silver to
weigh down his pockets. But though he feared this sorrow,
he said nothing of it to Secret, who padded after him, as close
to his heels as though he were Christopher's shadow. Faithful

Secret, still lost, still lorn, but always where Christopher could reach out with his hand and catch the warmth of his friendly fur.

Then one day, when the sun was at noon in the sky, there came the sound of many dogs barking. Secret left Christopher's heels and took to a tree. Christopher looked up the road. Running toward him were four dogs, the like of which he had never seen before. They were black, with sharp noses, and their curly hair was cut and trimmed into ruffles about their necks and legs. The dogs were followed by a large, gaily painted van, and the van was drawn by eight Shetland ponies. But the wonder of the procession was that on the back of each pony sat a monkey. There was a great noise, for the dogs were barking at the tops of their lungs, and the monkeys added their squeals to the general hubbub. Now that the cart was coming nearer, Christopher saw that there were two vans, one tied behind the other. A tall, dark man walked beside the ponies, cracking his whip and shouting to silence the dogs. Christopher stood stock-still, blinking his eyes to be certain that this was not a dream he was having. The dogs rushed to the trunk of the tree that hid Secret. When the two carts came alongside of Christopher, the man called his ponies to a halt. A boy, some years older than Christopher, sat on the driver's seat, holding the reins that guided the ponies.

"Good day, sir," said Christopher, timidly. "My cat's gone up that tree. Will you please call off your dogs?"

"I certainly will," answered the man, shouting so as to be heard over the gibbering and barking of monkeys and dogs. He walked to the back of the second wagon, and opened the doors. "Bon-Bon! Juliette! Suzanne! Simon!" he called, and the dogs came at his command. Then the doors of the cart closed upon them.

"Joseph," the man called to the boy, "we'll put the monkeys in while we are about it. They have had a good sunning." The boy jumped from his seat and scrambled among the little ponies, while the monkeys climbed on his back and head, and clung about his waist, and pulled his ears, jabbering all the while. But Joseph seemed to know just what to do, and the monkeys were shut in the cart with the dogs very shortly, and the road was quiet once more except for a muffled yelp now and then.

Christopher looked at the dark man, staring at his long, strange, and beautiful face. It was a face that looked as though it had not quite stiffened. There was a fluid look about it. Joseph, the boy, stood by the man now, his hands in his pockets, smiling at Christopher. Christopher saw that the man was the boy's father.

"Are you a circus?" Christopher asked, after thanking the man for calling off his dogs.

"No," he replied, "but we are little brother to a circus. See?" And he pointed to the words painted on the side of his van. Christopher walked around the van, the better to read them.

"MONSIEUR BO-BO'S FAMOUS DOG AND PONY SHOW," it said.

"I am Mr. Bo-Bo," the man said, "and this is my son, Joseph."

"And I am Christopher Tree and that's my cat, Secret," said Christopher, pointing to the top of the tree where Secret still crouched, not daring to come down.

Then Christopher stared and stared, not being able to think of anything further to say, though his mind was busy thinking what a fine thing it would be to travel about the country in these gay wagons, as Joseph and his father did. And on the heels of this thought came another. Christopher squeezed up his courage, and spoke.

"Have you any work that I could do, Mr. Bo-Bo?" he said. Mr. Bo-Bo smiled at him.

"Can you juggle balls, or ninepins, or perform any tricks of that kind?" he asked.

"No," said Christopher, "But I can climb things."

"Christopher," said Mr. Bo-Bo, "I wish we could take you

with us, but you see, as it is, there is just enough to keep Joseph—he is the ringmaster—and myself—I am the clown— and the animals. Unless you can do something that is part of the show, I think we cannot take you with us. I am sorry, lad. Good luck to you." And he held out his hand to Christopher.

Christopher's heart sank. To have met so splendid a person as Mr. Bo-Bo, and to lose him again, without so much as a chance to see his Famous Dog and Pony Show! It was the most bitter of all disappointments he had met on this road to seek his fortune. He swallowed hard once or twice, and then put his small hand into Mr. Bo-Bo's. When he trusted himself, he raised his eyes to Mr. Bo-Bo's face. But Mr. Bo-Bo's face was filled with a great look of astonishment. He was looking over Christopher's head, his eyes wide, his mouth open.

"Joseph!" he shouted. "*Regarde le chat!* Look at the cat!"

Christopher turned. It was Secret. He stood in the middle of the road, on his hind legs. He marched around in a circle, one-two, one-two. He saluted, paw and ear. He turned somersaults and paw-springs. He danced a jig. He performed all those magical, secret feats that he had performed on that far, May Day night. Mr. Bo-Bo and Joseph stared with amazement.

"Lad! lad!" said Mr. Bo-Bo at last. "Why have you not told me that you have this performing cat? That is marvelous! That is a wonder! But he is so clever. You shall join our show, of course." He was so excited by this time that he was turning around in circles. He rushed to Christopher, and caught him up in his arms, lifting him free of the ground. He kissed him, soundly, once on each cheek. Then Joseph rushed to him, too, and kissed him in the same manner as his father had. And when that was over, they all looked at Secret. He was sitting in the middle of the road, washing his left hind leg, which was sticking straight up in the air. He was unaware of all the excitement he had created.

Mr. Bo-Bo lifted Christopher up to the seat of the cart. Secret followed him, and sat on Christopher's lap. Then

Joseph and Mr. Bo-Bo clambered aboard, Mr. Bo-Bo still talking.

"Christopher," he asked, "how have you found this cat? How have you taught him these fine tricks? It is wonderful, I tell you. He will make our fortunes, that little cat!"

All this while Christopher had said not a word. What could he say? Fortunately Mr. Bo-Bo was so pleased and excited that he gave Christopher no time to answer his questions. Joseph shook the reins now, and the wagons lurched and started down the road. Mr. Bo-Bo's eyes were shining, and at last he burst out singing. It was a French song. When Joseph joined in the chorus, Christopher, sitting between them, bent his mouth to the shape of Secret's ear. "Thank you, Secret," he said. "Thank you, little changeling cat."

SECRET BECOMES MR. TIDY PAWS

Christopher discovered that one of the vans was reserved for the dogs and the monkeys, and the other was the home of Monsieur Bo-Bo and Joseph. The animals were stowed away comfortably in the various cages and boxes, and there was a little stove in their wagon. If the evening was cool, Monsieur Bo-Bo built a fire there, "Because," he said, "my monkeys, they are tender in their chests."

The van that served as home and shop for Mr. Bo-Bo and Joseph contained two bunks, built along the side, and a little stove for cooking, hung about with copper kettles and a long-handled warming pan. There was a chest of drawers in one corner of the wagon, and a table hinged to the wall, and a great clutter of hoops, bells, pieces of leather, saws, hammers, and a hand organ. There were boxes, too, stored with costumes, and lengths of material, and hats, and queer-shaped shoes. Joseph cleared away a little space on the crowded wall for Christopher, and he hung up his new calico shirts and his good suit of clothes.

For three days after Christopher joined the show they rode

down the highway, sometimes walking beside the dogs and the ponies, sometimes riding, letting the ponies pull the full burden for a spell. At night they camped by the way, turning the ponies to pasture, letting the dogs settle themselves among the three blanketed figures that slept about a little campfire. But before the sleeping there was the evening meal, and after the meal there was storytelling.

Christopher told the story of Bean Blossom and Mr. Jeremiad. Joseph told the story of Ali Baba and the Forty Thieves, but Mr. Bo-Bo told how he had once been a clown in the circus in France, and also many tales about the animals he had known. And he always ended the animal stories by saying: "But never have I seen anything as clever as your cat, Christopher. Tell me, how have you taught him all these things?"

Then Christopher did not know what to answer, because he remembered his grandmother's saying, "In matters of this kind, it is wise not to let your tongue know what your eyes have seen."

"Secret knew the tricks when he came to me, Mr. Bo-Bo," Christopher said, "I didn't teach him."

"Ah, now you joke with me, Christopher," said Mr. Bo-Bo. "That little cat, it is not only his name that is Secret, eh?"

On the fourth day they came to a village, and Mr. Bo-Bo said that they would give a performance here. Then Christopher's heart sank to his boots. For what was he to do? Could he be sure that Secret would perform every day, at a certain place, at a certain hour? He spoke to Secret about it.

"If you would let me know, Secret, that you understand." But Secret sat on Christopher's shoulder, looking upon the world with his strange yellow eyes, as if he understood nothing, as though he cared for no one. He jumped to the ground, however, stretched himself, and then fell to washing behind his ears with great vigor. Then Christopher knew he could depend upon him, for one does not wash behind the ears unless in preparation for some great event.

There was a park in the center of the village. It was there that Mr. Bo-Bo, with Christopher's help, raised up the red-and-yellow canvas tent, tying it with ropes to stakes driven in the ground. Joseph went about the town with a sheaf of posters under his arm, and these he nailed up on walls and fence posts so that everyone would know that Monsieur Bo-Bo's Dog and Pony Show had come to town.

Mr. Bo-Bo said he thought Christopher and Secret should have a rehearsal. Christopher, knowing how Secret would dislike it, said: "Mr. Bo-Bo, if we leave Secret to himself, I'm sure he will do just as he did in the road that day." Mr. Bo-Bo agreed, and it was decided between them that Christopher was to walk around the ring, turning handsprings and somersaults, and that Secret was to follow after, performing the same tricks, as though he were aping Christopher.

"And now," said Mr. Bo-Bo, "you must have a costume, Christopher." And he took Christopher to one of the large boxes where the costumes were kept. There was not one costume that was complete, though there were many pieces and bits. They decided that Christopher was to be dressed as a gypsy because little sewing need be done for such a costume. Mr. Bo-Bo said: "With the needle, Christopher, I am nothing. But with scissors and shears—ah, that is another matter." So by cutting off brown trousers, and slicing down the sleeves of a yellow blouse, and tying a piece of scarlet wool about his neck and waist, Christopher did look like a gypsy. Mr. Bo-Bo hung a large gold ring over one of Christopher's ears and covered the other with a silk handkerchief wrapped about his head.

"There!" he said. "That is splendid. Now. We make a little clown's hat for Secret, eh?"

Christopher knew that the lorn Secret would never consent to wear a clown's hat.

"Must he wear it, Mr. Bo-Bo?" asked Christopher. "He's too proud a cat to dress as a clown." Christopher was sorry he had spoken, for he knew that Mr. Bo-Bo himself was a

clown. But Mr. Bo-Bo only smiled, and said: "Ah, that is because he does not know what a great thing it is to be a clown.
Well, we will make him a little collar, for I have a piece of
fine Spanish leather, bright red, and I'll hang it about with
eight silver bells. How is that, Gypsy Christopher?"

"He will like that, Mr. Bo-Bo," said Christopher.

"Then fetch me his neck, so I may fit it."

Christopher went in search of Secret, and found him sleeping on the driver's seat. When he returned to the wagon, Mr.
Bo-Bo was hammering little silver bells into a strip of bright-
red leather, making them fast with small, brass-headed nails.
It was a rare and beautiful collar, and when they had fitted
it on Secret's neck, Secret walked away proudly, shaking himself to set the bells a-jingle.

"One more thing, Christopher," said Mr. Bo-Bo, "and that's
Secret's name. It's a fine name for you and me to call him by,
but for his public appearance I think he should have another."

Christopher remembered that once his Gran had called
him Mr. Tidy Paws. "Would 'Tidy Paws' do?" he asked.

"Splendid!" said Mr. Bo-Bo. "He is Mr. Tidy Paws, in the
ring."

MR. TIDY PAWS GIVES A PERFORMANCE

The villagers gathered about the tent soon after noonday,
waiting for the show to begin. Joseph was already dressed in
his long, blue, tight-fitting trousers, and his bright-yellow
coat, with a tall silk hat on his head, such a hat as the
wicked Mr. Jeremiad had worn when he first came to Bean
Blossom. Joseph was calling out all the wonders of the performance that were to be seen within the canvas walls of
the tent, and shouting to people to buy their tickets early.

Christopher, with Secret in his arms, was huddled in a
corner of the wagon, which they used as a dressing-room,
shaking with fright as he heard the voices and the shouting

children. He looked out miserably from the door of the wagon, and saw the eight ponies standing impatiently, their red harnesses bright in the sun, the feathered pompons standing erect on their foreheads. The dogs were barking wildly, and running in circles about the wagon. Everyone was eager for the show to begin, performers and audience alike —everyone but Christopher. Mr. Bo-Bo came leaping into the cart to get himself ready. He saw Christopher there, looking very sad and frightened.

"A little frightened, eh?" he said. "You need not be, Christopher. It will be splendid. When the people see Mr. Tidy Paws they will laugh, Christopher, and then your fears, they will go *pouf!* like a big bubble." Mr. Bo-Bo interrupted himself long enough to pull a white stocking over his head, leaving his face and his ears free. Now he painted his face white with a chalklike paint. "To hear the people laugh!" he said. "Ah, Christopher, that is worth all the work we do, all the long roads we travel, all the wind and rain that pound against our wagons. Laughter! It is like a song inside of you. You do not understand, Christopher? But you will. It is better than money in your pocket, or food in your belly."

Mr. Bo-Bo painted a large red mouth on his face now, and circled his cheek bones with dabs of red paint. He spread his face in a grin. It made Christopher laugh to see him. He dropped his head, then, and looked down his nose with such an air of sadness that Christopher felt the tears coming to his eyes. He saw, then, what it was about Mr. Bo-Bo that made his face beautiful and soft. It was because he used it in many different ways, sometimes for joy, and sometimes for sorrow. He dressed himself in a stiff white costume, the trousers wide and baggy, the coat decorated with bunches of ruffles at the neck and wrists. He put upon his feet huge yellow shoes that were seven times too large for him, and then, on top of his stockinged head, he put his tall, clown's hat.

"It's time to go, Christopher," he said, jumping from the wagon to the ground. Christopher followed him, still holding the silver-belled Secret. Mr. Bo-Bo gave one last glance at the ponies, and called to the dogs to be still. "Quiet, now," he said to them. "Rest a little, now." He took Christopher by the hand and walked with him to the entrance of the tent.

The hand organ was playing. Christopher and Secret, standing at the entrance, saw Joseph, in a little cart drawn by two of the ponies, circle the sawdust ring. He stood up as he rode, playing the hand organ. It was the sign for the performance to begin, and all the people settled quietly into their seats, and the chattering stopped. Joseph leaped from the cart and stood in the center of the ring.

"Ladies and gentlemen," he announced, holding his tall hat in his hand and making a fine sweep with his arm. "We now present Monsieur Bo-Bo, the great French clown." Mr. Bo-Bo ran into the circle, and the people clapped their hands, welcoming an old friend once more. Bon-Bon, the French poodle, followed him, yapping at his heels. Mr. Bo-Bo pretended to be frightened of the dog, and ran from him, pausing now and then to kick an immense foot in his direction. Everyone laughed. Mr. Bo-Bo fell and rolled over and over, tumbling about the ring, and Bon-Bon jumped over his tumbling body, knowing just how to space his jumps. At last Mr. Bo-Bo caught him with both feet, and Bon-Bon sat up on the broad soles of Mr. Bo-Bo's shoes, his tongue hanging out, his tail wagging.

The ponies came into the circle, with Joseph as ringmaster. They formed in many patterns, marching around in groups of two or three, changing their direction at the crack of Joseph's whip, rearing up on their hind legs, shaking their heads till their harnesses jingled. And all the while the hand organ played, with Joseph turning it when Bo-Bo was performing, and Bo-Bo turning it when Joseph held the center of the ring.

Now Bo-Bo brought out red and yellow hoops, and Suzanne and Simon ran through them, jumped through them, chased their own tails, and performed all manner of splendid tricks. Bon-Bon did likewise, but Juliette, the mischievous clown, did nothing that the others did. She pretended to jump through the hoop, but just when she should have jumped, she turned, and walked around it. And Bo-Bo stormed and scowled, though everyone knew that Juliette's mischief was part of the show. Once she disappeared completely. Everyone looked for her, the dogs, Bo-Bo, and Joseph. They found her. She was hiding in Joseph's silk hat, which he had put down on the ground for a moment.

There was a race between the dogs, too, with the monkeys for jockeys. Round and round the ring they ran until Mr. Bo-Bo declared Simon the winner and presented him with a little horseshoe of flowers.

Joseph stepped forward and beat upon a drum. When everyone was silent he said: "Ladies and gentlemen. We now present the most marvelous animal performance ever shown in any dog and pony show. Christopher Tree, and his performing cat, Mr. Tidy Paws. Ladies and gentlemen, your attention, please!"

Christopher knew that his time had come. Bo-Bo was there behind him. "Stout heart, Christopher," he whispered. Christopher felt his knees shaking. "Secret," he whispered, "Secret, are you there?" He cast one look behind him. Secret stood there, silent and proud. Christopher began his journey around the sawdust ring. Sharp with fear, his ears caught the little sound of Secret's paws and bells behind him. Christopher stood, and saluted. A ripple of laughter greeted him, and he knew without turning to look that Mr. Tidy Paws had saluted too. Christopher held his scarlet-sashed stomach, threw back his head, as though he were laughing. A shout of laughter went up now, and Christopher knew that Secret mocked him with furry paws and furry belly. Christopher turned handsprings, his fear gone from him now, and he heard behind him the jingling of Secret's silver bells as he turned on his little paws. Now the people were shouting with laughter, and calling out: "Look! Look at the cat!" "Can you see him, Mother?" "David, can you see the cat?"

They rose to their feet and stretched their necks with looking.

Suddenly Joseph changed the tune on the hand organ. It was quicker now, a lively song. Secret stepped to the center of the ring, without a sign from Christopher, and fell to dancing his jig. He spun about like a top. The children jumped up and down on their seats at this, and threw their hats and caps into the air, and one deep voice called out "Bravo! Bravo for the cat!" Everyone took up the cry. "Bravo!" they cried. "Bravo for Mr. Tidy Paws!" And the clapping of hands was like the sound of thunder. Long after the dance was done the clapping continued. Christopher and Mr. Tidy Paws had to bow many times before the people let them leave the ring at last.

That night Mr. Bo-Bo said: "We do not cook our dinner tonight. No, we go to the inn and are waited upon, like people who have nothing to do but amuse themselves, for this is a great day." To the inn they went, where Mr. Bo-Bo ordered a feast of roast chicken and garden peas, and a glass of ale for each of them. Mr. Tidy Paws went, too, curling up on the chair behind Christopher. The innkeeper, seeing the three of them sitting at the largest table, came up to them.

"I know you," he said to Mr. Bo-Bo, "for I saw your show this afternoon and I think your cat, lad, is the rarest thing I have ever seen." And he patted Christopher on the shoulder.

"You see," said Mr. Bo-Bo, when the innkeeper had left them, "it is just as I told you. The cat will bring us great good luck. His fame will spread about the countryside, and this summer's ending will find us heavier in pocket than we have ever been." He lifted his glass. "I toast Mr. Tidy Paws," he said. But Mr. Tidy Paws was beyond hearing all that was said of him. He was fast asleep, paw over eye.

BEAN BLOSSOM AGAIN

It happened just as Bo-Bo said it would. Secret's fame spread before the caravan, and whenever they arrived at a village, the children came running down the road to meet them.

"Is this the show that has the performing cat?" they asked.

"This is the show," Bo-Bo replied. And like as not, when the performance was given in the afternoon, there, on the front seats, sat the same children who had welcomed them on the road.

Christopher was proud of his changeling cat. But Secret himself was unaware of his spreading fame. Bo-Bo said: "That Secret, he is a great fellow, for he looks on success with the same eyes as he used before. There is no change in him." Then Mr. Bo-Bo drew a fine picture of Secret saluting, and this they used as a poster. And beneath Secret's picture were printed the words:

MR. TIDY PAWS

The World's Most Famous Performing Cat:

WITH

Monsieur Bo-Bo's Dog and Pony Show

Joseph nailed these posters up on the walls and fences, as he had done the others.

It was a splendid life altogether, and Christopher was happy with the animals, the days and nights on the road, the campfires, and Joseph and Mr. Bo-Bo. But one afternoon, as the caravan creaked down the road, Christopher saw that the goldenrod was waist-high in the fields, and when they drove down a wooded stretch of road, he saw that the silver birch trees were yellow and the sumach crimson at the tip.

"Mr. Bo-Bo," he said sadly, "I shall have to go back to Bean Blossom now, for the autumn has come."

"I know," said Mr. Bo-Bo. "Joseph and I spoke of it last night. We must be turning the carts to the south, where the monkeys may be warm through the winter." That night, after their supper, which they cooked on the stove in the wagon because the evening was very cool, they sat about the hinged table, studying the map.

"We will give two more performances, one here and one here," said Mr. Bo-Bo, tracing the places with his long finger. "Seven miles further we will come to the crossroads. A day's walking will bring you to Bean Blossom, Christopher, and Joseph and I take the other road and travel to the south."

The day came when the crossroads loomed up, early in the morning. Christopher and Joseph and Mr. Bo-Bo sat on the seat of the cart like three old crows, not speaking a word for sadness. At last Joseph broke the silence: "Come with us, Christopher," he said.

"No," said Christopher, "for I cannot leave my Gran."

"Never mind," said Mr. Bo-Bo. "We will all meet again, for good friends come together again no matter how far the earth stretches between them. If we do not come this way next year, we will the next; and then, if Secret is willing, we'll take to the road again. And now for your wages, Christopher." Mr. Bo-Bo jumped from the seat of the cart to the ground, and went back to open the doors of their wagon. Joseph and Christopher followed, climbing sadly up the little ladder stairs that led from the ground to the wagon. Mr. Bo-Bo took two leather bags tied with red string from the chest of drawers. "There are two," he said, "one for you, and one for Secret." Christopher saw that both bags were like to burst with money.

"Thank you, Mr. Bo-Bo, and thank you, Joseph," he said.

"No thanks to us, Christopher," said Mr. Bo-Bo. "Secret earned it, and what's more he filled our pockets, too," and he showed Christopher that his own leather bags were fat with money.

"Good Secret," murmured Christopher, and they all

turned their eyes to Secret, who was sitting in the door of the wagon, staring out upon the world. Christopher went down the little ladder for the last time, and said his farewells to the ponies. Joseph took him to the animal wagon, and Christopher stroked each monkey and spoke to each dog, thinking how sad it was that this summer's days had come to an end.

Then Christopher held out his hand to Joseph, but Joseph kissed him on both cheeks as he had done once before. Monsieur Bo-Bo said: "Christopher, I have bought a new shawl that I wish you to take to your grandmother." He gave Christopher a soft and many-colored shawl. "Her plaid one we have worn out. Give her my greeting. And long life to you, and to Secret Tidy Paws, to your good Gran, and to Bean Blossom." After this long speech he kissed Christopher on his cheeks, and then rushed to the seat of the driver's cart, where Joseph waited for him. He gave the signal to the ponies. Christopher saw the wagons lurch and turn, hiding the driver from his view. He watched that gay caravan dwindle away, into the morning sun, until it was just a blur in the distance. "Good-by," he cried, "good-by."

Christopher turned toward Bean Blossom, for when one sorrow is left behind, like as not there's joy on the road ahead. He and Secret walked that day in great content. First the sky looked familiar, then the road, and then each tree—maple, birch and elm—took on the look of something known. Evening brought them once more to the poplar-lined road down which they had disappeared that summer's day. There was the house, standing alone and proud, in the deserted village. Christopher ran. It was dusk, now. As he ran he saw the candlelight go up against the windowpane. His Gran was there.

"Gran!" he shouted, "Gran! It's Christopher," knowing that his voice would be home before his legs could carry him there. His Gran opened the door.

"Christopher!" she shouted. "Hurry, hurry, my darling!" And then he was burying his head on her shoulder. "And

Secret with you!" she said. "I'm glad for that. I dreaded your homecoming for one thing, and that was that Secret disappeared the very day you left home."

"He's been with me, Gran," said Christopher, trying to tell her everything at once. "And he's made our fortune." They were in the cottage now, Gran having shut the door on the darkness. Secret walked about the house, sniffing every corner, settling down by the fireplace at last.

"Christopher, how well you look! How tall you've grown!"

"Where's the teapot, Gran?" Christopher asked. Gran brought out the old blue teapot, and took off the lid. Christopher untied his two leather bags and sent a stream of coins rolling into the pot. They clattered merrily against the china walls. They covered the bottom of it, they piled up the sides. It was more than half full.

"Christopher! How did you get so much money?" his Gran asked.

"Secret got it. Is there enough, Gran? Enough to keep us in Bean Blossom for a year?"

"Enough!" said his Gran, "why, Christopher, that teapot is holding flour, and corn, and a new roof for the barn and one for the house, and an overcoat for you. Oh Christopher, this will keep us in Bean Blossom for many a long year. How did you do it?"

"We joined a dog and pony show, Gran. And Secret was the star performer. Do you remember that May Day night? Well, he performed every day, and sometimes twice a day, all the things I saw him do that night. And he had his picture painted. And people came for miles around to see him. And . . . oh Gran, I don't know what to tell you first."

Betsy Tree suddenly came to her senses. "First we shall have our supper," she said, "and afterwards you and I and Secret will sit before the fire, and you shall tell me the whole story, from the beginning."

They did as Betsy said. And after supper, Betsy, taking out her knitting, sat with bright eyes, listening to Christopher as he told the story of Secret and his spreading fame. Now and then Betsy looked at Secret, sleeping by the fire, and broke into Christopher's tale to say "Good Secret!" or "Now the darling Mr. Tidy Paws!" Once she bent her head close to Christopher and whispered: "But you told no one about his being a changeling cat?"

"Not a soul," said Christopher.

"Good," said Betsy, "for you may be sure the little people like their secrets well guarded. Oh Christopher, you are a wise boy, so you are." She said this with such emphasis that her ball of sky-blue yarn spun out of her basket and across the floor. Secret woke with a start, and bounded after it as lively as a kitten. He pounced upon it, with a great curved leap. Christopher looked at him with astonishment.

"Gran," he shouted. "Look at Secret. Mr. Tidy Paws is gay! Oh, Gran, he's home with us at last." And so he was!

The Daring Young Man
on the Flying Trapeze

EDWARD FENTON

Robin hung head down from the trapeze bar in his room. He was unkinking.

He had been in Herr Liedvogel's back room most of the day, working on his somersaults and cutting cleaner the line of his flying movement. His muscles ached a little now that the day was over, but it was a pleasant kind of weariness. He knew that he had not only worked hard, but well. His somersaults were getting more nearly perfect every day, so the ache didn't matter.

There was a stubborn knot of muscles in his shoulder, how-ever, and another in his thigh. It eased them when he swung gently from the trapeze.

It also seemed to help him think.

Ever since the previous night there were a couple of mental knots that had to be straightened out, and they were as hard as those in his shoulder and thigh. He was racking his thoughts to think of some way to help Mrs. Fatima, some scheme to get enough money to save her house. So far he had only two ideas. One involved the daring rescue of the son (or daughter, if necessary) of a millionaire from under the wheels of the Flatbush Avenue trolley car. The other was the finding of a purse full of uncut diamonds, or a satchel lined with ten-dollar bills.

Unfortunately, both these plans had their essential difficulties.

As he turned over the bar Robin decided that such things never really happened to anyone, anyway, except in books and movies. Nothing he thought of seemed sufficiently practical. And he kept seeing the look on Mrs. Fatima's face when she took Herr Liedvogel's arm and led the way into the parlor. He would never forget it as long as he lived, he told himself; and he had to do something to change that look. That was all there was to it!

But it would have to be before October. And what could *he* do?

The other knot was Uncle Theodore. Now that he was coming back, Robin would have to tell him about his flying. Robin wanted Danilo's approval and encouragement more than anything else in the world. If only Uncle Ted would let him fly, he thought, he would be so good that even Danilo the Dauntless would be proud.

Mrs. Fatima had told him not to worry about it. "I'll have a good long talk with him first thing," she had said, smiling confidently at Robin.

But Robin knew that Danilo's resolve was as firm as a tent stake driven into the ground with a twenty-pound mallet. Robin had seen it often enough to know. There had been the time of the accident, for instance. Even though it had hurt unbearably, Danilo had gone on with the act until the lights faded on his final bow. From the wings Robin had watched his uncle gritting his teeth so that he could bear the pain, clamping his jaws so hard that his neck muscles bulged.

Robin had always admired his uncle's strength of will, but now it troubled him. Was there anything that could make Danilo change his mind? Robin doubted whether even Mrs. Fatima could succeed.

And Danilo's return was only a couple of days off. Robin couldn't wait to see him again; they had been apart so long, and there was so much to tell him—except for this one thing. It shadowed everything he did like a dark rain cloud over a summer's day, or like—yes, like the sea gull hovering over his drifting rowboat in the dream.

He was suddenly too tired to hang from the trapeze any longer. He let himself down and got into bed. He couldn't read tonight. He turned off the light, and up from the street came the casual, clear, familiar noises of the summer night: an auto horn; high, young voices giggling around the lamp post at the corner; the jangling of the bell from an ice-cream vendor's cart; a distant trolley car rumbling along on its tracks. Somewhere someone was pounding a piano, practicing "Over the Waves." The tune went on, over and over, seemingly endless, filling the hot summer night.

It had happened on a night when Hooker's Circus played a small town in Oklahoma. Ever since the matinee showing, Danilo's shoulder—the one he had injured before—had been bothering him. But he didn't pay any attention to it. It was nothing, he thought: only a touch of the weather.

He was in his dressing-room getting ready for his call when a sudden sharp twinge shot through him. But it was too late to do anything then, or even to give it more than a fleeting thought. At that minute the important thing was to give a show.

He could hear the opening bars of his music. Hastily he rubbed talcum powder on his hands and dashed into the arena.

Everything went well until halfway through the act. He had just been completing his somersault when it came. He didn't know what was happening. Because of the pain which tore through him he couldn't even see what was before him. And then—

Danilo smiled as he repeated the story at the supper table, as though it weren't anything very important or serious— only something wryly amusing that had happened to him on tour, along with a lot of other things.

And then he had missed the catcher's outstretched waiting hands, and he was falling, cutting through the bright, gaudy space of the tent, cleaving the sharp beams of the spotlights. There was no net. He fell to the sawdust ring below.

Through the confusion he heard the ringmaster shouting that everyone was to remain seated, please! A troupe of clowns ran hurriedly out from the wings and pranced about to divert the audience while Danilo was being carried out of the tent on a stretcher. The band played furiously, and the next act rushed on.

The circus doctor had said that it was a miracle he was still alive.

They left Danilo the Dauntless in Tulsa.

He spent what seemed to him forever in a hospital bed, and the show went on its way. He recovered quickly, but at the hospital they told him that although he could leave, it would be a long time before he could walk without his crutches. He could never hope to fly again, they told him.

"Well," he said cheerfully, "it's all part of the job. I guess I was lucky, really. I can't complain."

Then he told them hilarious stories about his friends, Little Lillie, the Fat Lady of Hooker's Circus, and her husband, Mister Spook the Living Skeleton, until the whole dining-room rocked with laughter.

But all during supper Robin was very pale and quiet as he sat beside his uncle. There was the bowl filled with Mrs. Fatima's wonderful spaghetti, and the crisp green salad, and the blue picture plates, and all the special festivity of a Thursday night at Mrs. Fatima's. But for once Robin could not enjoy any of it. It seemed impossible that all these things could remain the same and yet his uncle be so changed.

He sat numbly, remembering all their happy times together. He thought of how he used to stand in the wings tingling with pride as he watched Danilo the Dauntless perform. And afterward they would go around the corner to some eating place where they would pitch into ham and eggs and coffee and discuss the show with the other artists before going back to the hotel to sleep. He remembered the brass beds and the artificial potted palms and the traveling from town to town; and he thought he could never be as happy again as in those lost-past days with his Uncle Theodore. He thought of them longingly; and at the same time he was ashamed of having been so happy then. If he had known then! If he had only known, he told himself, he would have treasured every moment while it was still happening!

And now it was all over. Danilo the Dauntless would never fly again. Never again would he take a bow at the end of a show in the wonderful way he had, while everyone clapped their hands and shouted bravo! The spangled tights of the Danilo who had been so truly dauntless were folded away at the bottom of a trunk. Robin hardly dared to look at his uncle's face now. He was afraid of the change that he might find there as well.

The meal was over at last. Everyone was standing. Herr Liedvogel proposed a toast.

"You all know to whom," he said. "And I guess I don't have to tell anyone here how brave and courageous he is, and what a splendid performer. Ladies and gentlemen, I give you —Danilo the Dauntless! Ja, and I also give you our Theodore: an old trouper and a good friend!"

And after the toast was drunk Mr. Ellery Crane began to sing:

> *For he's a jolly good fellow,*
> *For he's a jolly good fellow,*
> *For he's a jolly good fe-e-llow—*
> *Which nobody can deny!*

Everyone joined in.

Finally the singing and the toasting were over and it was time to go into the parlor. Uncle Theodore fumbled behind his chair for his crutches and led the way with Mrs. Fatima.

Later, as soon as he could, Robin slipped away. He wanted to be alone. He ran upstairs to his own attic room where he stayed, lying quiet in the darkness, listening to the sounds of music and singing and laughter which came floating upstairs from below.

Then, in the darkness, the poem from the blue book of *Gems from the Muse's Diadem* crept into Robin's thoughts:

> *Joy and woe are woven fine,*
> *A clothing for the soul devine;*
>
> *Under every grief and pine*
> *Runs a joy with silken twine. . . .*

But where was the joy with its silken twine now? Robin got up from his bed and washed his face, wondering, as he went through the mechanical motions of getting ready to go to sleep, if he would ever find it anywhere.

The next morning there was a crispness in the air when Robin woke up; a clear edge of the weather which was almost like autumn. By the time he had finished his breakfast it had dissolved and was gone again. But Robin knew that the long summer was beginning to draw to its end.

At ten o'clock he appeared as usual at the bakery. His face was set and tight. When he faced the door of the practice room with its sign: STRICTLY PRIVATE THIS MEANS YOU, he wondered for the first time if it did mean him, too. The world of flying, of bars and ropes and somersaults, lay behind that door. KEEP OUT, it said. THIS MEANS YOU.

Robin had to swallow hard before he could make himself turn the familiar knob and go in.

August was seated on his neat bed, playing the flute. His cheeks were very puffy and his face very red. His eyes were focused on the music rack in front of him.

The door closed behind Robin with a click. August stopped playing and squinted at his watch.

"Just on the dot," he said, smiling.

Robin nodded and didn't say anything.

Herr Liedvogel picked up his sheets of music from the stand and waved them. "Well," he said, beaming, "today we start flying with music. How do you like the idea?"

"I don't know if—" Robin began uncertainly.

"*Du lieber Gott!*" roared the Great August. "We can't stand here and *klatsch* all morning! You just go and put on your tights and come right back."

"Yes, Mr. Liedvogel," Robin said.

When he returned in his practice clothes, August announced: "And now I will first play the music through once so you can hear how it goes. It begins with the introductions, a sort of slow waltz. So." He raised the flute to his lips and played the introduction. "Then the main music comes in, all a variation on one theme." He played the theme through. It was very simple, with an easy, swinging rhythm. Then he repeated it, playing it over and over, each time varying it slightly.

Robin stood beside him, staring ahead.

"And now," Herr Liedvogel commanded, pointing upward with his stubby finger, "you climb up and show me! Go ahead. Don't be afraid to make mistakes. Only fly!"

The introductory bars began. Obediently Robin ascended and swung back and forth with the slow waltz. Then, tentatively at first, he followed the music with flying figures. By

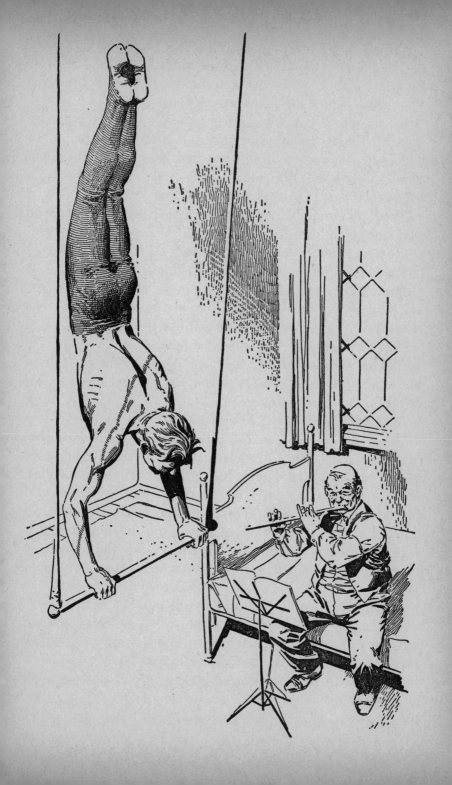

the third variation his confidence had grown and his move-
ments were certain. As he turned and flew, he found himself
creating variations of his own to go with the music.

Herr Liedvogel was blowing hard, but at the end of the
fourth variation he stopped just long enough to shout up,
"Bravo! Wonderful!" then he was furiously blowing away
again.

Robin was about to swing out once more when suddenly
there was the flapping of the sea gull's dark wings about his
ears, and he had a vision of a burly figure climbing up the
steps of Mrs. Fatima's house. The figure went painfully, on
wooden crutches.

It paralyzed him. It was as though he were stuck in mid-
air. Below him Herrr Liedvogel's face snapped back and
forth like something in a nightmare. The notes of the flute
whirled shrilly up to him. Then they stopped.

The next thing he was standing on the floor, breathing hard
and clinging to the rope with his sweating fists. He hardly
knew how he had managed to get down. The palms of his
hands burned.

"But it was fine!" August cried. *"Gott in Himmel,* why did
you stop?"

"I don't know," Robin said, a little dizzily. "I just—I just
did, I guess."

Herr Liedvogel regarded him with concern.

"You didn't hurt yourself?"

Robin shook his head.

"Then tell me: what was the trouble?"

"I don't know," Robin said. "I had to come down. I felt
sort of funny. I'm all right now, I think."

But Herr Liedvogel knew that he wasn't all right. He gently
fisticuffed the boy's jaw. "You were doing fine up there," he
said slowly. "I was proud of you."

"Thanks, Mr. Liedvogel," Robin said. The floor under his
feet didn't feel altogether real. He couldn't be quite sure
whether he was still in the air or standing on the canvas mat.

"How about going up and trying it once more?" Herr Liedvogel suggested.

Robin only shook his head dumbly.

"Just once, eh? It was so beautiful until you stopped. Come on. *Hup!*"

Robin didn't move.

August put his hands on the boy's shoulders. He felt them quiver involuntarily at his touch. "You were afraid, yes?" he asked quietly.

Robin remained with his eyes fixed on the mat. He was numb inside. There were no words with which to answer.

"But why? Why? Because of Danilo?"

Without looking up from the mat Robin nodded uncertainly.

"Listen to me," August said earnestly. "No matter where you are, there is danger behind you: crossing the street, sailing on a boat, riding on the subway, or even flying from a trapeze. But you have to forget about it if you want to fly! Was Leotard afraid? Or Blondin when he went across Niagara Falls on a thin wire? Or any of the great ones? And tell me this: was Danilo ever afraid, even after his accident?

"No," he went on. "Because they were all great artists, above the crowd, and they weren't afraid. When you first began to fly, you first learned to beat gravity and dizziness and then you conquered space. But before you really begin to be a performer, you have to learn to calculate your risks and take them for granted. But I can't teach you that. The only one who can teach it to you is yourself. And you will, too. I have spent my whole life watching artists, and I know how it goes. You have come so far. You mustn't stop now. You can't turn back."

There was a long moment of silence.

"Ach, words!" Herr Liedvogel cried impatiently. "How can I show you with words? Listen: if you want to, you will do it. Nothing will stop you. But you must learn now!"

With his heart still clenched by fear, Robin thought of the

dark bird and the way its wings beat the air. He remembered the dream: the oars slipping from his grasp, and the dreadful silence.

Then he saw something else: the white tips of the gull's wings and the snowy place on its breast. Mrs. Fatima had said that she was sure they meant something. What was it she had said? "White stands for faith."

Robin looked up into Herr Liedvogel's face at last. He knew now what the dream meant.

"Suppose you come back tomorrow," Herr Liedvogel was saying. "We'll try it once more with the music then, yes?"

"Yes, Mr. Liedvogel!" he answered. "We'll try it again tomorrow. And it'll be O.K. tomorrow, too. You just wait and see!"

In the days that followed there were times when Robin felt as though he were treading solidly on clouds. Those were the times when he felt so close to his goal that he could almost, he thought, touch the very sky, and nothing could stop him. But the next day he would leave the bakery with a sinking heart, desperate of ever succeeding.

Herr Liedvogel was never surprised. "*Ja*, that's how it goes," he said cheerfully.

Mrs. Fatima, meanwhile, helped to allay Uncle Theodore's suspicions by pretending to send Robin off on errands every morning. It was safe enough. Uncle Theodore seldom left the house.

He hated to be stared at when he made his hobbling way along the street, and so for long hours he sat in the parlor window with his crutches on the carpet beside him and the latest issue of *Billboard* spread open on his lap. Sometimes he stared through the potted ferns at the people passing in the street.

Mrs. Fatima came and sat with him whenever she could. Often they were very gay together so that the emptiness left his eyes and for a while he was able to escape from his own faraway thoughts. Sometimes they were joined by Mrs. Fatima's mother-in-law, who knew how to tell as good a story as any she heard. And frequently he went upstairs to the second floor to have tea with the ex-Queens of the American Traveling Stage.

In the evenings, after their work was done, Herr Liedvogel and the Delicatessen Man sometimes came to see him. They liked to sit in his room drinking Celery Tonic and talking about the good old days and how things had changed since then. Now and again, in the middle of a story, Danilo might stop abruptly to stare unseeingly straight ahead of him, arrested by some secret thought that passed across his mind to draw him back into the past. It never disturbed his callers, though. They went on sipping their tonic and waited until he was ready to go on with the story.

Robin often spent the evening with him in his room, talking about everyday happenings at Mrs. Fatima's. When Uncle Theodore was in a good mood he would recall funny things about Hooker's Circus, and tell Robin how the act had gone over, in different towns. Or else Robin read aloud while his uncle quietly sat and listened. As often as not he looked as though he were listening intently, but Robin knew that he was really lost among his own reflections.

One night his uncle said abruptly: "Put that book aside for a while, Rob. I haven't really gotten around to having a serious talk with you since I got back."

Robin said "Sure, Uncle Ted," and there was a pause after that.

"It's been on my mind a lot lately," his uncle said. "You see, it won't be long before fall now, and we ought to start hunting up a school for you. It's time we started to make some plans for your future." Danilo tried to smile, and looked wryly down at his crutches. "I don't want you to turn out the way I did."

"Gosh, Uncle Ted, don't talk that way!"

"Well, you ought to begin thinking about what you'd like to do. Have you any ideas?"

"I haven't really thought of anything special," Robin said lamely.

"At any rate," his uncle remarked, "I suppose you can see how idiotic it is to fly around in a circus tent. That's one thing I'll bet on not catching you doing, eh? Feet on the ground, that's the motto for our family from now on!"

Robin didn't say anything.

"You see, my boy-o," he continued, "this sort of life is all very well in its way, but it's not regular. There's no stability to it. It's not right for a youngster like you to be growing up among a lot of show people, and see nothing but cheap dressing-rooms, and boarding-houses, and shoddy hotels. You've had plenty of that already, and it's not what I want for you. I've seen a sight too much of it myself. And what does it get you? Look at me. I'm all finished, and what do I have to show for all these years? A couple of smashed pins and a pair of crutches and a trunk full of stuff that I never want to lay eyes on again."

"I wish you wouldn't talk like that, Uncle Ted. It gives me the gollywoggles."

"It's true enough, though," said Danilo sadly.

Robin shook his head. He said: "I'd sooner be you, Uncle Ted—I mean I'd rather have been Danilo the Dauntless than any lawyer or engineer or—or anything!"

Danilo looked into his nephew's grave eyes. Then he laughed bitterly.

A moment of unbearable quietness followed. Robin broke it finally. "Let's finish this story now, Uncle Ted," he said. "We can talk about schools and stuff afterward. There's lots of time, Uncle Ted, really there is!"

He quickly opened the book and began to read in a loud voice.

The summer was drawing to a close, but Robin hardly noticed the change in the days. He needed more hours than they held. Every moment he could spare he spent before the great mirrors of Herr Liedvogel's back room. For hours on end he worked tirelessly: practicing, correcting, improving, polishing—and then practicing all over again.

His fear was not all gone. But he was learning to overcome it. Each time, he noticed, Herr Liedvogel's smile was a little broader, and the pleased twinkle in his eyes came more readily.

The following Thursday night was a gala occasion. Mrs. Fatima's spaghetti and salad had never been better. When everyone adjourned to the parlor, Mrs. Fatima's mother-in-law sat herself down at the piano and struck some tentative chords.

"It's a long time since we've had 'Just Break the News to Mother'!" She hummed the opening bars with satisfaction. "I shall sing it now," she decided. And she did.

Everyone joined in the doleful chorus, and her hearty baritone boomed above them all:

> *Just-ah say there is no other*
> *Can-ah take the place of Mother,*
> *And tell her noooooot to wait for me,*
> *For-ah I'm not coming hooooooooome! . . .*

"My, that's a pretty piece," said Lydia Ellen. "And it's real affecting, too!"

Right after the second chorus the doorbell rang. Lydia Ellen pulled herself together and went out to the vestibule to answer it. When she reappeared, a man stood behind her on the parlor threshold. He had on a white linen suit with a sky-blue shirt and tie, and the Panama hat which he held in his hand had a sky-blue band to match.

"Why, Dick Bendix!" Mrs. Fatima cried. "Come right in. We saw in *Billboard* that you were back in town. This *is* a treat."

"I happened to be passing by, so I thought I'd pop in to see how every little thing is coming along," he explained.

"And I'm glad you did! Robin, get Mr. Bendix a strong

chair, and Lydia, you get him some coffee and a good-sized slice of Mr. Liedvogel's layer cake."

Everyone was in good form that night, from the Delicatessen Man's violin solo right on through. By special request Madame Moré repeated her famous Renunciation Speech from *Camille*, and the Signora followed with the Sleepwalking Scene of Lady Macbeth. Long before she had finished Robin could feel the flesh creeping along his spine.

As the very last attraction, Paul and Virginia, the seals, did their celebrated rhumba. It was better than ever, and needless to say it brought down the house. It had to be repeated three times before everyone was satisfied.

When the applause finally died away, Mr. Bendix rose to say good-by.

Mrs. Fatima said she hoped he'd come again.

"Oh, I hope to return very soon," he answered. He exchanged a look with Robin.

"Let me see you to the door, Mr. Bendix," Robin said.

But Herr Liedvogel, at his elbow, cut in. "Don't bother, my boy," he said. "I'll show Mr. Bendix out." And he marched Mr. Bendix to the vestibule.

When he returned, Robin saw that his Toby-jug face was lit with a broad grin. Robin wondered what he or Dick Bendix could have said in that short time to make him smile like that.

Breakfast the next morning was fairly tense. It was the day for the decision about Paul and Virginia.

Mrs. Fatima's mother-in-law sat in her place looking very stiff and righteous, while Lydia Ellen passed the plates and waited on table enfolded in conspicuous and significant silence. Robin was glad when he had finished his milk and could leave the table.

He went to Herr Liedvogel's early. The baker seemed very busy behind a pile of fresh rolls, so Robin went into the back room by himself, changed his clothes, and began to practice. He felt that he was going to work well this morning.

He had just completed a perfect somersault when he heard the door open. He looked down for a moment. It was Herr Liedvogel, and he had someone else with him. When Robin saw, after a moment, who it was, a quick glow tinged his face beneath its film of sweat.

He did not stop to greet them, however, or show that he had seen them come in. Instead, with a clean, beautiful precision he went through the air and turned a somersault. His muscles obeyed him perfectly as he flew from trapeze to trapeze. And as he flew he became oblivious of their eyes upon him. He was thinking only of what he was doing, concentrating all he had on that miraculous co-ordination of time and space which makes up a trapeze act. He felt as though he could go on flying up there forever.

When he finally came down, August was beaming. Dick Bendix was looking at him interestedly, through narrowed eyes. But now that he was on their level, facing them on the floor, Robin was suddenly shy. He rubbed his hot palms along his tights.

"Hello, Mr. Bendix," he said. "You—you weren't supposed to come *here!*"

"No, sirree, but since Mr. Liedvogel here extended me a special invitation last night, I thought I might as well take advantage of it. And I'm not so sure but what it wasn't worth the trouble."

Robin felt the Great August's cold, firm fingers on his forehead, pushing back his curling damp hair. He knew that August was proud of him.

In the shower the water poured over his body with a rushing sound. He stood there and closed his eyes, and it sounded almost like applause. He could already see the great yellow rings of the circus while he flew far above them in the eaves of the tent.

Mr. Bendix walked back to Mrs. Fatima's with him. Now

that they were outside on the pavement Robin felt a strange uncertainty come over him. Dick Bendix wasn't saying a word. If only he'd say something, Robin thought, instead of just frowning to himself that way!

They had come to Mrs. Fatima's flight of steps.

Mr. Bendix, no longer frowning, turned and gave Robin a hard, calculating look, as though he were testing with his eyes every muscle in his body and every ounce of endurance he possessed. Then he said, grinning: "Well, I guess you've got something . . . !"

That was all he said. But it made all the difference. Robin climbed the steps happily to Mrs. Fatima's front door.

No sooner had they appeared in the doorway than they realized that a major crisis was taking place. Lydia Ellen's face was a tragic mask, streaked with tears.

"Well, what's the Sweeney woman been up to now?" Mr. Bendix demanded, trying not to smile.

"Oh, Mister Bendix," she sobbed, "I ain't done nothing this time, but they're going to take away Paul and Virginia and baby Charleymane and put them in a zoo! But if they goes, I goes. But I don't want to go, and I don't think I'll ever smile again, ever!"

"And why do they have to go to a zoo?" Mr. Bendix wanted to know.

Lydia Ellen's wails started afresh. Mrs. Fatima sighed. Her mother-in-law countered with: "I don't *want* to send them away, young man. But if you must know, Mrs. Fatima simply can't afford to keep them here any longer. Why, she isn't even sure she'll be able to keep herself here! And somebody, even if it is myself, has to be commonsensical in this household. And let me tell you, young man, that's no snap!"

"But why shouldn't they be able to earn their keep—and more?" he asked.

Mrs. Fatima's mother-in-law regarded him with profound skepticism through her bifocals.

Robin held his breath and waited.

"There's that rhumba I saw them do last night, for instance," said Mr. Bendix mildly. "I think I could use that in the show. I've been looking around for something to fill a certain spot. I don't see why I shouldn't use those seals of yours for it."

The air had suddenly cleared. Mrs. Fatima was beaming. "Hooray!" Robin shouted wildly. And Lydia Ellen, whose hysterics had turned off as though with an electric switch, stood wreathed in smiles, blinking incredulously.

"Oh, my! And am I going to be in it, too?"

"That's right, Lydia!" Mr. Bendix said with a laugh. "Now you just slip upstairs, get into your best bonnet, and put some powder on your nose. Because you're coming along with me to my office and we'll draw up a contract right now."

"Are we going in a taxicab?" Lydia Ellen asked, wide-eyed.

"I can see no reason why the expense wouldn't be justifiable!"

She blinked again. "A taxicab! Did you hear that, Mrs. Fatima? A real taxicab. Please, Mister Bendix, could you make it a yellow one with an open top? Oh, dearie me, I'll be right back!" She ran out of the room. After a moment she could be heard calling to the seals: "We're going to be stars!"

They were everywhere, it seemed. Mrs. Fatima's mother-in-law reported that in the course of one trolley ride she had counted six big pictorial billboards on as many vacant lots, with three-foot lettering on them, announcing:

DON'T MISS IT!
BENDIX'S BIG SHOW
ONLY THREE DAYS IN BROOKLYN
STARTING NEXT TUESDAY
SEPTEMBER THIRD

No one at Mrs. Fatima's could talk of anything else. And no one had the least intention of missing it. Mr. Bendix had sent Mrs. Fatima tickets for a whole box in the special reserved section for Tuesday night, and they were all going.

Several times a day Lydia Ellen put Paul and Virginia and Charleymane the Second through their paces. They rehearsed with enthusiasm.

"I bet they know what's going to happen Tuesday!" Lydia Ellen told Robin.

Robin, however, spent less and less time at Mrs. Fatima's as the day of their debut grew nearer. He was at Herr Lied- vogel's most of the day, practicing. When he was home he avoided Danilo's searching, unhappy eyes. Each day the hedge which kept them apart seemed to have grown more impenetrable.

Meanwhile, the pages of Mrs. Fatima's kitchen calendar were ripped off, one by one. Friday: tuna fish and green peas. Saturday: fried chicken and mashed potatoes. Sunday: roast beef, with pistachio ice cream for dessert. Monday: cur- ried veal and green beans. And the next morning when Robin woke up he said to himself: "It's today!"

He was a little surprised to see, when he looked out of the window, that it was just like any other day.

Lydia Ellen started things off by losing her glasses again, in spite of which she went downstairs for a fresh henna rinse. "I got to look my best tonight," she explained. "Everybody will be looking!"

But when the rinse was over and she surged into the kitchen, all steamy and flushed from the effort, Mrs. Fatima took one look at her and gasped.

"Heavens above, Lydia Ellen Sweeney, what have you done to yourself? You should have squinted harder at that bottle. Because instead of Madame Gigi's Henna Rinse you've gone and done your hair with Sophy's green-and- yellow paint!"

Lydia Ellen fled to her room. There were her glasses, right on top of her dresser pincushion. When she put them on and beheld in the mirror the full effect of her altered appearance, she vowed that nothing would ever get her to set foot out of her room.

Mrs. Fatima hurried upstairs to her old theatrical trunk and rummaged about in it. When she had found what she was looking for, she called: "Stop crying this minute, Lyddy! Come up here and try this on."

It was a purple turban threaded with gold constellations and sewn with huge pearls and glass rubies. It had a great diamond sunburst in front, complete with spreading rhinestone rays.

Lydia Ellen gaped at it. She was enchanted. The turban reeked of Mothine, but as far as she was concerned, that was merely part of the glory.

"Oh my, Mrs. Fatima, thank you!" she breathed, as she tucked the last wisp of apple-green hair under its opulent folds. And it was not Lydia Ellen Sweeney who proceeded to make the beds and dust the parlor that morning, but Sheba's Queen in All Her Splendor.

Supper was served early. Everyone was there, even Mrs. Schultze, the Delicatessen Man's wife, who had bribed a neighbor's daughter to stay with little Frieda. She had brought along Gunther and Hildegarde and Otto, and they all sat in their places very scrubbed and quiet and awed. Mrs. Fatima's mother-in-law was, as usual, very stately in her black lace; and as for Mrs. Fatima, Robin had never seen her look so lovely. She was wearing a long dress of soft blue and her gold forget-me-not brooch and gold evening slippers.

Somewhere during the course of the day Lydia Ellen had got hold of a tall aigrette which she had tucked into Mrs. Fatima's purple turban. It now rose above the glittering sunburst like one of the fountains of Versailles in full play. Lydia Ellen was obviously very pleased indeed with her own appearance.

The last to enter the dining-room were Bella Figlia and Della Moré. Their entrance was greeted by an awestruck silence, and those ladies accepted it as no less than their due.

They had on long white gowns, heavily embroidered with beads; and as they entered the dining-room, their trains were just leaving the hall staircase. Madame Moré wore her long diamond earrings, a rhinestone dog-collar, and a tiara of rhinestones blazing in her hair. Rhinestone buckles glittered on her pumps. In one hand she carried a gold mesh bag, while with the other she wielded an enormous fan of white ostrich feathers.

The Signora's only jewels were her Tecla pearls which cascaded down to her waist. However, her ostrich fan was, if anything, even more enormous than her friend's. And although it was a warm evening, over one arm she carried an ermine stole tufted with little black tails.

"Well, my dears," the Signora announced triumphantly, "*we're* ready!"

Before supper was over a florist's box was delivered at the front door. It held flowers for all the ladies, with Mr. Bendix's card.

"A perfect gentleman, I always did think so!" pronounced Mrs. Fatima's mother-in-law as she pinned on the corsage of yellow tea roses that had been sent for her.

Bella Figlia and Della Moré each had two gardenias tied with silver ribbon. Lydia Ellen's flowers were red roses. "Oh my! They're American Beauty roses, and they got ferns all around!" She was quite dizzy for a moment. "Oh, if only Charleymane Finnegan was here!" she said wistfully.

Last of all there was a bunch of fragrant violets for Mrs. Fatima, and with them a card which read: "For the Bendix Show's greatest Star—with gratitude."

"Wasn't that gallant of him!" exclaimed Mrs. Fatima. She looked thoughtful, and Robin wondered if she was remembering Dick Bendix's father and the time she had saved the show for him in Milwaukee.

Then the doorbell rang again.

This time it was the taxicab that was to take Lydia Ellen and the seals to the circus grounds. It was yellow, too, and it had an open top! The aigrette on Lydia Ellen's turban bobbed perilously as she descended the steps to enter the cab, and all Wistaria Street was running out onto the porches and leaning out of the windows to witness the departure of Lydia Ellen and the seals for their debut.

No sooner had the neighbors all gone inside, thinking that the excitement was over, than three more taxicabs drove up along the curb in front of Mrs. Fatima's house, to take Mrs. Fatima and her party to Bendix's Big Show.

If Lydia Ellen's appearance had created a sensation, that of Signora and Madame caused what amounted to an ovation. But they simply gathered up their trains and stepped haughtily into their taxi, looking neither to the right nor to the left. Not for nothing had they impersonated queens and duchesses and countless great ladies in all their years on the stage. "Drive on, young man!" commanded the Divine Sarah Bernhardt's Greatest and Only Rival. "And don't dilly-dally!" added her companion, with a superb wave of her hand.

Uncle Theodore was in the last cab with Mrs. Fatima and her mother-in-law.

"You're coming along with us," Robin heard him call through the window.

Robin stood on the sidewalk, hesitating.

"I think I'll walk, Uncle Ted," he answered. "I know the way. It isn't far."

"What?" cried Danilo. "You come with us!" But the door slammed shut and the taxi shot forward, following the others. Robin watched it turn the corner. Then he started to walk.

He walked quickly. It was a lovely night, clear and gentle. It was just beginning to get dark, and the moon shone like a bright new dime in the palm of the sky.

As he went along he thought of how, when he had first come to know Mrs. Fatima, he had hoped for a fire so that he could rescue her from the flames. He smiled. He knew now how he could show her how much he loved her without calling out the whole fire brigade! It was a harder way, perhaps, but it was a better way. And it was more—special. If only he didn't fail her now, he thought desperately. But he knew that he couldn't fail, because it was no longer something that he wanted to do for himself alone, but for Mrs. Fatima.

As he proceeded through the darkening summer night, lost in his own thoughts, he suddenly became aware that a band was playing. The music became louder as he went on. He turned a corner, and then, there it was.

It was breathtaking, like having a dull-looking book fall unexpectedly open at a wonderful picture in many colors, or like peeping through the window at one end of an Easter egg. There were festoons of colored lights strung across the sky; and a brightly lighted carrousel with pawing Arabian steeds going around and around; and a huge Ferris wheel with electric lights strung along its spokes like pearls. There were booths with popcorn and lemonade and hot dogs and kewpie dolls. And behind them all loomed an enormous golden tent. A huge sign said "BENDIX'S BIG SHOW," and as Robin stared up at it, he saw the silver-dime moon shining above everything.

When Mrs. Fatima's party arrived, most of the seats in the tent were already filled. Curious eyes watched them as they settled themselves. Their neighbors paused with popcorn halfway to their mouths, conjecturing as to who the new arrivals might be.

Danilo peered anxiously around for Robin.

"I don't know what's come over that boy," he muttered. "It's not like him to—"

"I think there he comes now, Theodore," August interrupted. "Do you see him over there?"

"Where?"

At that moment, however, it was impossible to make sure. The lights in the vast tent were dimming. There was a burst of music. The show had begun. The parade was coming into the tent.

Robin watched from the rear. He saw it all through a haze. The clowns, the animals, the sequined costumes all swam in front of his eyes. The resounding *oompah! oompah!* of the band sounded somehow very far away.

Then, when the parade was over, he stood like someone in a dream and watched the whirling acrobats, and the elephants in their lugubrious dance, and the living statues going through their stately measures. He watched the equestrian acts and the clowns again and the lion-tamers cracking their whips in their cages. He watched Mrs. Fatima's friend, Samsonetta, bend iron bars across her powerful back and hold four men suspended in the air from a bit held between her teeth; and he watched Signor Rastello, magnificent in a blue-and-gold uniform, juggling more things than Robin could count, keeping them dancing up in the air, seemingly forever.

When Signor Rastello had finished, a blue-and-red platform was wheeled out into the ring. It was for the seals. Robin felt his heart pounding against his ribs in excitement as Lydia Ellen waddled proudly into the tent followed by Paul and Virginia and Charleymane the Second. And then, not a bit disturbed by the vast audience, the seals jumped up onto the platform, just as though they were right in Mrs. Fatima's parlor on a Thursday night.

They warmed up with a game of ball. That was followed by a selection on the mouth organ, which won great applause. And finally the band began to play a rhumba.

In a flash they had wriggled into their Cuban costumes, and while Charleymane the Second held a Cuban rattle in his mouth, shaking it in time to the music, Paul and Virginia did their rhumba. Paul wriggled his ruffled sleeves in the air and Virginia coyly swished the flounces of her train from side to side. Back and forth they went, dancing more and more sinuously. By the time the music stopped, they had brought down the house. Robin had never heard such applause. Paul and Virginia bowed happily and waved their flippers at the grandstands until it was time for them to leave the ring. In the excitement Lydia Ellen very nearly lost her aigrette!

It was clear that Paul and Virginia and Charleymane the Second had joined the big show for good.

Then, while the clowns came out and capered, the platform was wheeled away and the ring was prepared for the next act. The lights were shifted and dimmed.

In the half-darkness, softly, the horns began to play a slow waltz. A bright spotlight was turned on. It made a great silver cone of light in the middle of the arena. Then another spotlight revealed the network of ropes and bars stretched across the roof of the tent.

The violins joined in, swelling the waltz as the audience saw a boy spring out of the wings. He had a little blue cap on his head and he was cloaked in a shimmering blue cape.

He bowed and dropped the cape, revealing a lithe figure in shining white tights. Then he began to climb. Up he went, and always higher, not stopping until he had reached the highest trapeze. The cape lay in a little blue pool on the ground below.

Then the horns began to play "The Daring Young Man on the Flying Trapeze," and out into the vast silvery space the boy swung.

No one breathed as his supple body flew from trapeze to trapeze. He was like something which had been created to fly.

Waiting and trembling, he had thought of Danilo the Dauntless and Herr Liedvogel and Mrs. Fatima—especially Mrs. Fatima. But now he had no thought for anything but what he was doing. This was his moment. He flew and whirled and somersaulted over and over, as though he and the music and the wonder would never stop, but would go on forever and forever in the bright shaft of light.

He flew on and on, never seeming to tire, following the music with endless variations. Each movement he made became more breathtaking than the one before.

Finally the drums rolled out brashly. The violins repeated the tune for the last time as he finished his final somersault. And then, as the very last note slithered into silence, he came down the rope and made his bow.

The whole tent was very still. For a moment nothing happened.

And then everyone suddenly came to life and the applause of the crowd began!

He bowed three times. After the third bow, the band picked up the cue for the Grand Finale and the Daring Young Man dashed out of the ring.

The show was over.

The next minute they were all milling about in the circus back yard. There was a great delirium of explaining and exclaiming and congratulating and hugging. Everyone wanted a share in the excitement.

Herr Liedvogel was there. He beamed proudly at Robin. "Ach," he said, over and over again, "you were so wonderful, my boy!" Uncle Theodore was there, too. There was an odd expression on his face.

Robin looked up uncertainly at him.

"So," Danilo the Dauntless said. "I thought our family was going to keep its feet on the ground from now on. But I guess it's too late to start now, eh?"

He was smiling in the old way that Robin knew so well, and his arms opened wide. Robin flung himself into them, and suddenly the high hedge between them had faded away and was gone.

Acknowledgment

The author and publisher wish to make acknowledgment of their indebtedness to the following publishers and authors:

Charles Coombs and Boys' Life, published by the Boy Scouts of America, for permission to reprint "Cat Man" by Charles Coombs.

Dodd, Mead & Company, Inc. for permission to reprint "Barnum's First Circus" from *Barnum's First Circus* by Laura Benét.

Doubleday & Company, Inc. for permission to reprint "The Daring Young Man on the Flying Trapeze" from *Hidden Trapezes* by Edward Fenton.

E. P. Dutton & Co., Inc. for permission to reprint "The Trained Kangaroo" from *Old Covered Wagon Show Days* by Robert Barton and George Ernest Thomas.

Don Lang for permission to reprint "Jenny and Her Pets."

J. B. Lippincott Company and Josephine Lofting for permission to reprint "Doctor Dolittle's Circus" from *Doctor Dolittle's Circus* by Hugh Lofting.

The Macmillan Company for permission to reprint "Breakfast with a Hero" from *All Over Town* by Carol Ryrie Brink.

Ruth Manning-Sanders for permission to reprint "The Bear" from *The Circus Book* by Ruth Manning-Sanders.

Story Parade, Inc. for permission to reprint "Oscar at the Circus" by Mabel Neikirk; and "Tinker of the Big Top" by Esther Van Sciver.

Noel Streatfeild for permission to reprint "Mis" from *Circus Shoes* by Noel Streatfeild, published by Random House, Inc.

The Viking Press, Inc. for permission to reprint "Mr. Tidy Paws" from *Mr. Tidy Paws* by Frances Clarke Sayers, with lithographs by Zhenya Gay.

DAT